W9-BJR-095

01/2012

THE BLUE SKY

GALSAN TSCHINAG

THE BLUE SKY

A NOVEL

TRANSLATED FROM THE GERMAN
BY KATHARINA ROUT

MILKWEED
EDITIONS

© Suhrkamp Verlag, Frankfurt am Main, 1994
© 2006, translation by Katharina Rout

Published 2006 by Milkweed Editions
Originally published as *Der blaue Himmel* by Suhrkamp Verlag, Frankfurt am Main, 1994.
Printed in Canada
Cover design by Christian Fuenfhausen
Cover photograph of boy by Peter Langer
Cover photograph of landscape courtesy Sergey Turgenev
Author photo by Amélie Schenk
Interior design by Percolator
The text of this book is set in Anziano.
06 07 08 09 10   5 4 3 2 1
First American Edition

Milkweed Editions, a nonprofit publisher, gratefully acknowledges sustaining support from Emilie and Henry Buchwald; Bush Foundation; Patrick and Aimee Butler Family Foundation; Cargill Value Investment; Timothy and Tara Clark Family Charitable Fund; Dougherty Family Foundation; Ecolab Foundation; General Mills Foundation; John and Joanne Gordon; Greystone Foundation; Institute for Scholarship in the Liberal Arts, College of Arts and Sciences, University of Notre Dame; Constance B. Kunin; Marshall BankFirst; Marshall Field's Gives; May Department Stores Company Foundation; McKnight Foundation; a grant from the Minnesota State Arts Board, through an appropriation by the Minnesota State Legislature, a grant from the National Endowment for the Arts, and private funders; an award from the National Endowment for the Arts, which believes that a great nation deserves great art; Navarre Corporation; Debbie Reynolds; St. Paul Travelers Foundation; Ellen and Sheldon Sturgis; Target Foundation; Gertrude Sexton Thompson Charitable Trust (George R. A. Johnson, Trustee); James R. Thorpe Foundation; Toro Foundation; Serene and Christopher Warren; W. M. Foundation; and Xcel Energy Foundation.

The publication of this work was supported by a grant from the Goethe-Institut.

Library of Congress Cataloging-in-Publication Data

Tschinag, Galsan, 1943–
[Blaue Himmel. English]
The blue sky / Galsan Tschinag ; translated by Katharina Rout. — 1st American ed.
    p. cm.
ISBN-13: 978-1-57131-055-2 (hardcover : alk. paper)
ISBN-10: 1-57131-055-X (hardcover : alk. paper)
I. Rout, Katharina. II. Title.
PT2682.S297B5413 2006
833'.914—dc22

2006022865

This book is printed on acid-free paper.

NATIONAL ENDOWMENT FOR THE ARTS
Established 1965

MINNESOTA STATE ARTS BOARD

The publication of *The Blue Sky* is made possible in part through support from The Greystone Foundation, given in honor of George R. A. Johnson.

For my grandmother—
The warming sun at the beginning of my life

THE BLUE SKY

3   The Dream

11   Grandma

53   The *Ail*

85   Farewell

137   Arsylang

189   Glossary

193   Words to Accompany
my *Blue Sky* Child

203   Translator's Note

THE BLUE SKY

THE DREAM

This story may have begun in a dream. Was it a preparation for things to come, a warning perhaps? For it was a bad dream—a nightmare.

Don't ever tell anybody about your bad dreams, people said. Tell your dreams to a hole in the ground and spit three times. They said similar things about good dreams. Don't share them with anybody. Keep them to yourself. So, I wondered, were the only dreams you ever heard the dreams that were neither good nor bad?

We usually started the day in our yurt by telling each other what we had dreamed the night before. Oddly enough, it made everybody both happy and worried at the same time, which you could tell from watching the listeners.

But when I had my dream, I didn't know that rule. So while the dream was hot, as hot as tears, I passed it on to my mother. I had cried and had to be woken up. It was Mother who had woken me. She had come into the yurt from the morning milking to empty the full pail, and the hand that stroked me was wet and cool and smelled of raw milk.

Still sobbing, I told her what I had just dreamed. But after she listened to my story, she announced it was a good dream. I wondered if she was really listening because while I was talking, she was busy straining the milk through a tuft of yak tail hairs into the big aluminum jug. "No, it was not!" I said fiercely and started sobbing again. Mother held her ground. What's more, she said my interpretation of the dream was wrong, and talked instead of gold, silver, and silk, of celebrations and sweets. None of it made sense to me.

But I learned: Don't tell your dream to anybody, tell it to a hole in the ground, and spit three times.

That's what she explained when she turned back at the door. "Mind you, that's only for a truly bad dream!" she warned.

Of course it was a bad dream. So I had to do what had to be done. But I had already shared it with somebody, with Mother. What now?

I thought about it as I crawled out from under the old, quilted coat that had once belonged to Father and was now my blanket. And I was still thinking it over as I set off into the new day.

A bright summer morning welcomed me with the smell of dew, sun, and animal pee. Just then the flock of sheep was noisily leaving the pen, while the lambs stayed tethered to the *höne* and formed a square, white patch. The women and girls were milking the yaks at the *dshele*. All around me squirts of milk were drumming into pails of resonating aspen wood; each sounded different, from a bright hiss to the dark gurgle of water bubbling up from an earth eye.

Our dog Arsylang was asleep next to the dung-heap. He was breathing peacefully. Sunlight streamed onto his dark, downy fur and exploded into rays that glittered and danced on the ends of his hair. His ribs rose and fell almost imperceptibly. His limbs lay slightly curved and gathered in as if they had neither joints nor weight. I could see his body was calm, and everything was as it had been: good. But what about the dream?

I went over to Mother, who, squatting beside a cow, milked it so nimbly and vigorously that her shoulders rocked as if they were trembling. She had buried half her face in the cow's thick, bushy belly fur and had closed her one, still-visible eye.

I moved my mouth close to her ear and whispered: "Mother!" The eye opened. "What if you have already told somebody?"

Mother didn't immediately catch what I meant. She had to think. Then she said firmly: "Don't ever tell anybody about your dream. Not anybody!"

I got scared and left. I thought more about it and decided it was not yet too late to run out into the steppe and get rid of the dream. Somehow it seemed better than leaving the matter all wrong.

I walked a fair way from the *ail*. Then I turned to face the mouth of the river valley and spoke, enunciating each word as clearly as I could: IN MY DREAM, MY ARSYLANG HAS BEEN POISONED. HE CANNOT WALK OR STAND. HE STAGGERS, FALLS OVER, AND FOAMS AT THE MOUTH. HIS LIMBS ARE STIFF, HIS FUR STANDS ON END, HE IS DYING. OH-OH-OH!

Just then the dogs raced off, barking noisily, to chase a horseman who was speeding at some distance past the *ail*. When he noticed the dogs coming closer, the horseman slowed from a gallop to a trot and then slowed even further until he rode at a calm walk. The dogs reached him, raced around him in circles, and barked at him. But they soon calmed down, and eventually they lost interest in the placid horseman and turned back.

Under the morning sun, which was still low in the sky, I dallied and played with my long, thin shadow, trying to catch up with it, but never getting lucky. No matter how quickly I skipped, the shadow leapt along and always got away. Then the dogs returned. With their tails curled high above their backs, they walked lazily, yawned, and licked their mouths with their long, dangling pink tongues.

But not so Arsylang. He never curled his tail, nor did he lift it much, but carried it slanting downward, with its tip only slightly curved outward. And his ears rose straight up; pointy like a foal's and close to each other, they looked like a pair of scissors. He was ambling as usual, his neck reaching forward, with the collected poise of a predator.

Arsylang was a foundling dog. When he was still a pup, Father had brought him from far away. At the time the pup came to us, I already had my first teeth. But the young dog grew fast and had long been considered grown up, while I was still a child.

Nobody who came to visit us ignored Arsylang. Everybody acknowledged him with at least a general comment: "Oi, that's a dangerous dog." To which the reply was always the same, regardless of who was helping the guest off his saddle or lifting him back up again: "He only looks that way."

Arsylang was not dangerous and had never bitten anybody. But people never stopped fearing him. Usually, their remarks would lead to a longer conversation about the dog.

Some people commented on his name, which meant

"lion." Then Father would reply that the lion's job was not to see but to hear. Others said we should not have called the dog Arsylang, but Börü, which meant "wolf." To which Father would answer: "That would mean calling the wolf by its name ten or twenty times a day and drawing it near—who would do that?"

Suddenly I felt like seeing Arsylang run. So I ran backward and called out in one breath, "Arsylang, Arsylang, Arsylang!" and then, "Tuh-tuh-tuuh!" Here and there barking rang out, and all of a sudden the dogs came charging. I watched how Arsylang ran: he stretched and pressed low to the ground, his tail flat and straight. He tore past the dogs that had taken off ahead of him, and he was now in the lead. I ran a bit further and crouched beside a burrow that a marmot or maybe even a fox could have easily slid into. When Arsylang arrived, he landed with his muzzle right in the burrow and, whimpering and scratching with all four paws, tried to squeeze the rest of himself into it as well. Grass and soil, still damp from the night's dew, flew up in lumps. Then came a dry layer of soil which crumbled into dust and grew into a little cloud. I called Arsylang by his name, and he stopped straining. But the excitement wouldn't let go of him for a long time: He continued to whimper, and his fur stood on end.

I got a fright.

Then Grandma arrived. She walked toward me with little toddling steps. Because I didn't want her to drag herself so far from the *ail* for my sake, I called, "tshuh!", gave myself a slap on the bottom, and galloped toward her.

The dogs followed me. Arsylang soon caught up and trotted along beside me. The other dogs stayed behind, none passed us.

Grandma stopped. She had grabbed the top end of her short birchwood stick with both hands and was leaning on it when we reached her.

"What was that? Was it a wolf?" she asked softly, with that little smile on her lips that rarely faded. "No, not a wolf," I said, unsure of myself. "Maybe a fox or just a marmot." I felt a little hurt that Grandma would ask me a question I had to answer with a lie.

"Where have you been, Grandma?" I asked sullenly, partly to fend off the shame that was bound to come, and partly to counter that shame by keeping alive the feeling of hurt so I would find it easier, for the first time ever, to keep a secret from her.

"I had to relieve myself," Grandma said humbly.

"So long and so far away?"

"I went behind the hill. My legs are getting on."

Grandma sighed, but immediately cheered up again. She pointed at her legs: "I told the two of them, Don't be so lazy or I'll take you to herd the sheep!"

I didn't want to reply because I thought her joke was inappropriate. Instead, I wanted to get to the bottom of something else: "Grandma, why did you have to go behind the hill? The others squat right here in the steppe."

"Oh, I couldn't do that, dear. I'm not used to squatting while people look—I could never do that!"

Suddenly a fierce feeling for her overcame me. It was part compassion and part awe. Then it changed into love. It felt like pain, it really hurt. The rims of my eyes turned hot. "Grandma!" I said and took her hand. She looked at me so kindly and with such understanding that I could barely speak: "Let's go, Grandma. Let's go home."

GRANDMA

Grandma was human silk. That's what Father said, and what he said was always right. Always. And she had been sent to me by the sky. That's what Mother had revealed to me. Some of the things she said weren't true of course, but when the sky was involved, we were not allowed to lie. Mother had said so herself and even Grandma had listened.

At first she was a stranger among us, people said. She used to have a husband, a son, a yurt, and a sizeable flock. Later her husband was shot dead by fleeing Russians, and her son struck dead by pillaging Kazakhs. The two events happened one right after the other.

Left all alone, she sought the company of her younger sister, Hööshek. The sister was widowed as well, and for all I know, she was the only woman in our corner of the world who had managed to acquire the title *baj*. She had a son who, though long grown up, had remained weak and shy; and probably as a result of this worry Hööshek felt both more important as head of her family and more determined to assert herself in life.

Grandma did not talk much about her sister, and what little she said was good. She never said anything bad about anybody, not even about strangers. That's the way she was.

In spite of that, people talked a great deal about Hööshek and about what she had done with Grandmother's yurt and flock. The stories added up. They were common knowledge.

Hööshek and her family always kept their distance, and yet a story was put together one crumb at a time that added up to some kind of picture of what Grandma's life had been like at her sister's. Hööshek has long since died. It's believed in all languages and among all peoples that one must never speak ill of the dead. Why is that? Is being dead a luxury for the select few to enjoy? Or a punishment for outcasts to atone themselves? No, it is the price we all must pay for having been here, for the miracle worked with our birth. Let us therefore follow the trail of what happened and stay in the shining light of truth.

Piece by piece, Grandma's yurt and flock wandered

into Hööshek's possession. The good felt blankets were found to be much more useful covering the sister's yurt than lying around unused and going to rot. This followed on the heels of Hööshek saying, Why put up two yurts if one has enough room for all of us?

So Grandma had to let her own yurt sit as a pile of bundles and had moved into her sister's yurt. When the first of Grandma's bundles was fished out of the pile, unwrapped, and its blanket taken, the word was, Just for now, until we've rolled new felt and sewn new blankets! But new felt was never rolled, and then more blankets were taken.

Meanwhile even the poorer pieces of felt were used as saddlecloths for mounts and pack animals. At first they were taken whole, as makeshift, on loan for a short time, but not long after, they were cut and sewn to measure. The same thing happened with the wooden scaffolding. The roof ribs were taken first. One after another they were put to different uses. And it did not take long before Hööshek took liberties and casually hacked one of the ribs to pieces and turned it into stakes. Stakes, after all, were needed.

Later, parts of Grandma's lattice work, of her yurt's walls, ended up in Hööshek's yurt, replacing those of hers in need of repair.

Same with the animals. Hööshek now preferred to cover running expenses with lambs and kids, and at times even with mature sheep and goats, all from

Grandma's flock. Grandma's were runts anyway, not as good as Hööshek's flock. Better to keep one good flock, and one day Hööshek would replace Grandma's animals. But not a single lamb was ever replaced. Nothing ever was.

One day it was understood that there was no longer any point in dragging along from one move to the next a pile that had once contained a yurt. So the remains of the pile were broken up. Anything left of value was claimed, while the rest was burned on a fire. This is how Grandma became homeless. And if she had stayed with her sister any longer, she probably would have become destitute as well. Fortunately, things turned out differently.

People called Grandma *Dongur Hootschun*, which means "old woman with a shaved head." The name was accurate. She was the first of only two women with a completely shaved head that I have ever seen among our people.

By the way, the other woman, who lived in the Altai Mountains half a lifetime later, was also called *Dongur Hootschun*. And the nickname, as is often the case, had replaced Grandma's real name long ago. No one will ever know what she was called when she still had the long black hair that she kept in two braids. I myself called her *Dongor Enem*—my grandma with the shaved head. When other children tried to follow my example, I quickly told them off: "Why *Enem*? She's not your grandma, is she?"

In those days, the children in the Altai Mountains used to live in peace with one another. So the child I had just told off would likely respond: "Oh well, it's *Eneng* then—your grandma."

Father and Mother and the other grown-ups in the *ail* put my name in front of Grandma's and used the ending that indicates belonging, or rather possession. I liked that, for she was indeed *my* grandma. And this is how that came about: Since moving in with her sister, Grandma had taken care of the lighter chores in the yurt and the *hürde* because, having long passed seventy, she no longer had the strength for more. She rarely saw anybody, and even more rarely went—or rather, given her age—rode anywhere. She only went out when she wanted to get her head shaved, rather than get her hair cut, since the former trade was plied by men only.

So it happened that one day Grandma rode off again to find someone who would shave her head. On her way she passed our *ail* and our yurt. This is easily told now when in truth it was a bad story, albeit one with a good ending. Grandma's horse had shied at dogs and already raced past four or five *ails*. The dogs—there were three of them at first—stayed hard on the horse's and its rider's heels. Ever more dogs joined in, and in the end they made up a pack of more than a dozen. Our cousin Molum, who happened to ride past, saved her: He chased the fleeing horse until he caught up and eventually got hold of its reins.

Understandably, a guest who arrived in such a manner was offered a warm welcome. Still panting and shaking, the old woman was seated on the good felt mat, which usually stayed rolled up behind a stack of clothes and was brought out only for guests of honor or rare visitors. She was welcomed and pitied by the grown-ups and eyed with curiosity and wonder by the children. The children had come galloping, a whole horde, even before the visitor was helped off her saddle, while the grown-ups showed up one by one—the first one with her baby at her breast, the next one with the hide she was tanning, the third holding the piece of clothing she was sewing—each in turn repeating more or less what had already been said and asked. Grandma, too, replied to the questions and the gentle chiding with almost identical words—getting chided of course because she had been careless enough to get involved with a horse that wasn't docile.

Grandma's horse was a mare that used to have a dark gray coat but, getting older, now looked almost white. The mare was anything but wild, but had once been attacked and badly mangled by wolves.

Ever since, she had been shy of dogs. She foaled each year but the late-winter snowstorms, the wolves, and Hööshek all taken together had managed to ensure the mare remained Grandma's one and only mount.

On the stove, the best tea was being prepared. The best tea meant that in addition to milk and salt a very fatty, floury paste was added to the concentrated tea. The tea was the result of a communal effort. Each woman who had comfortably settled her girth between door and stove made herself useful. The curiosity of the horde of children grew with the smell of burning fat and flour. They could not wait to find out who this person was who had a man's head and a woman's voice. Because they were not allowed to enter the yurt like the grown-ups or even to stand in its doorway, they kept walking past the door to steal quick, inquisitive glances at the yurt's inside. That almost made them ache.

When the guest stepped over the yurt's threshold, a small, noisily babbling child reached for her. That was nothing special. In those days any child, as soon as it was able to move on its own and until it could tell danger from no-danger, was tethered with a rope to the head of its parents' bed. This way the child was protected from the many dangers it could get into. But much like a tethered young animal, a child subjected to the practice quickly grew bored and craved any form of companionship. And so the toddler flapped and chirped toward the entering guest, and the very first person to greet me was Grandma. At this point, she was to me still just an old woman with a shaved head, but she responded to my greeting in her own way. She nodded at me and caressed me from a distance, blessing me and wishing me a long life with the following words: "Take my white head, my remaining yellow teeth, and the years on top!" Then she had to take her eyes off me for a little while to exchange greetings with the grown-ups and to hold and sniff the snuff bottles she was offered along with the greetings. She herself did not take snuff.

Unable to leave her alone, I waved wildly and continued to make a racket, my eyes riveted to her the entire time. This went on until people took notice and decided to free me from the rope. As soon as I could, I made my way straight to her on all fours and with a joyous scream grabbed hold of the hands she offered me. She helped me to my feet, pulled me close, sniffed first my hands and then my hair, and again wished me a long life — this time she talked to the mountains and asked them: "Oh, my rich Altai! Take this tiny pup into your lap to protect him from below; take this tiny pup into your armpit to protect him from above, and grant him a long life with long-lasting happiness!" Then she took me into her lap and held me. And from that moment on she was no longer for me and my family an old woman with a shaved head but my grandma with the shaved head.

Grandma spent the day in our *ail* and stayed overnight. As she went from one yurt to the next to drink the tea people prepared for her, I was glued to her back. Until then, Mother had always torn pieces for me off the dumplings or pancakes in the bowls, but now Grandma did that for me. This went on until I was overcome by sleep.

The next morning Grandma's gray mare was saddled early, but she could not leave until around noon since I refused to get off her lap and started to scream each time people tried to pull me off her. She had to wait until I fell asleep again. Cousin Molum took her home, because of the dogs and also because of her sister. He carried with him a few words from Father and Mother. Once they arrived at Hööshek's yurt, he was to speak on behalf of Grandma.

Grandma returned in the spring. But before spring there was winter, and in those days people heard very little of each other during that long time. Often they heard nothing at all. That year my parents could not find out until spring whether the Höösheks in Baschgy Dag had had a winter with only a few losses, and whether Grandma had got through the winter.

Then she came! It was still in the lean time between the storms and the move, and our yurt had only just arrived at Hara Hoowu. The Höösheks were stopping over at Saryg Höl on their way down from the mountains into the steppe. Grandma praised Sedip, the Hööshek son and her nephew, for his sharp young eyes and his binoculars and asked him to keep an eye on Hara Dag, across the Ak-Hem. One morning Sedip announced that the *ail* was leaving. And then he followed the movements of the flock of sheep and herd of yaks with the loaded oxen, reporting to Grandma in short intervals: "Passing the Heritsche above Doora Hara. At Üd Ödek. In Gysyl Schat. Along the Ak-Hem."

"Keep watching, my dear," Grandma said, "we'll soon know where people are heading." Shortly afterward she learned that the herds were crossing the Ak-Hem toward the area above Gysyl Ushuk. And so Grandma knew where our yurt could soon be found.

The next morning she rode off to get her head shaved and freshened up, as she put it to her sister. She found our yurt where she had expected it. Mother chided her when she heard that Grandma had all by herself and with some trouble crossed the Homdu, the great and dangerous river. The ice covering was already full of holes and cracks, and Grandma said she had seen deep water in a few places. But of course Mother was also happy that Grandma had come. As for me, who in the meantime had grown and learned to walk, the same happened as before: With a scream I hastened toward her and climbed into her lap, determined never to leave again. I remained there and stayed awake till late in the evening. When I finally went to sleep, Grandma could have kept me at her side all night, but she passed me back to Mother. Grandma had not touched her hair since we had last seen her, and it had grown a lot. This way she always had an excuse ready to come to us.

The storms did not simply continue but grew worse with each passing day even as the sun, their counterforce, inevitably grew stronger as well. The clash of these two natural forces had a destructive influence on half the world, and the rivers' icy armor grew more brittle by the hour until it cracked and dissolved.

Father, who had abducted Grandma from me while I was asleep, brought her back in the afternoon. I felt as if the joy that had filled me when I saw Grandma for the first time had stayed inside me like some wave or like a breeze of light burning so intensely and radiantly that it blazed a bright trail through the time since I had last seen her. By now the river had become impassable since the cool of the night could no longer weld together for even a few hours the shards of ice that were breaking apart. The icy mass was like softened clay that sank beneath a horse's hoof. Father had no choice but to call out to one of the Kazakhs who in those days had already settled on the other side of the river to come to the bank, and to ask him to pass the word to Hööshek at Saryg Höl.

Grandma stayed with us until early summer. She was a big help in the household, mostly because she kept an eye on me. But it was more than that: she brought me up. She would not have thought of it that way, though. In those days, nobody in a yurt would have thought that he or she was "bringing up" a child, just as no child would have been aware that it was being "brought up." The word did not exist in our language.

Grandma loved being with us. All of a sudden, a little one had pushed his way into her motherly, long-orphaned soul, filling it with light.

Twice Hööshek's words reached us. Letters did not exist in those days, aside from those from far away, from soldiers. In the interior of the country we only had words which, as soon as they were spoken, were relayed from the mouth to the ear by people passing through. The first words Hööshek said and sent on their way to her sister were short and merely consisted of a statement and a question that probably contained an admonition as well: "The river has been passable again for quite some time now. Why haven't you come back?" Before these words arrived, others had been spoken in our yurt. Father and Mother had invited Grandma to stay with us. Father's offer had gone exactly as follows: "I carried my father away when he died, and my mother as well. Now I can stand tall before the sky and my children and say I have fulfilled my filial duties. But not all are granted the opportunity to fulfill their most sacred duty. The sky may know why that is. Since time immemorial people have done their best not to leave such duties unfulfilled. And whoever is allowed to perform this duty for another human being is a happy man. But the truth is that this right must be earned. *Awaj*, it is up to you to name the one you consider worthy to carry you in his hands the final distance when that day may come for you. Should your choice fall onto me, it would make me as happy as if my mother had returned to let me once again live with her for a while and then carry her to her final rest a second time."

Mother decided on the following words: "I am not good enough to be given the honor of caring for my mother in her old age. Others, better ones among my siblings, have been chosen to do so. But you shall know, *Daaj*, that you will be a mother to me if you can see a daughter in me. And this, too, shall you know: When there is tea in the tea pot, I will pour you the strongest sip, and when there is meat in the kettle, I will serve you the tastiest bit."

Grandma responded with similarly solemn words: "We were ten siblings to leap from our mother's body, but only two of us remain. Hööshek is the youngest. I could take on the mother's role for her, fulfill a mother's duty, and enjoy a mother's right. I am a bad person because so far I have only done so by halves. I am sure, therefore, that I have disappointed the spirits of Father and Mother and our siblings. How much worse would they feel if I abandoned my only remaining sister while we are still alive?"

This, then, was a rejection.

The second time Hööshek's words were more detailed and ran like this: "If your belly is fuller and your body more rested among strangers than they were when you were with me, your natural sister, then feel free to stay there until you die. But in my yurt and all around it lies stuff that is yours. I'd like to know whether to toss it or whether you still need it. When I moved to the summer pasture, your stuff gave me plenty of trouble, and I want you to know I'd rather save myself the trouble on the way back."

Mother, who was there when these words were delivered, called out in indignation: "She's talking about stuff? Why not talk about the animals then, too?"

But Grandma kept her calm and sent back the following words: "You were hatched by the same womb and grew in the same nest I did. Thus it is your duty to carry me into the steppe when my time has come. I now release you from your duty and ask you to carry away and burn instead of my corpse the things that belong to me. But save my underwear and the two *tons*. I will fetch them someday, when I get a chance, and later, when I'm dead, Schynykbaj and Balsyng will destroy them. And one more word: You spoke of strangers. To us, the Kazakhs, the Chinese, and the Russians are strangers, but they, too, are human beings. If you look more closely, you will see that we are kin even to the animals around us. Why then not kin to people whoever they may be? We are all shoots of one tree, children of one mother. Do not turn your siblings into strangers. This I can say because I have known things longer and also because my end is likely not far off."

The two people whose names Grandma had mentioned and whom she had appointed to destroy her things upon her death were my father and my mother.

With this, Grandma had made her decision.

What should happen with her livestock, however, had not yet been decided. She herself said nothing about it, which was rather odd. Father and Mother talked it over. Maybe Grandma was shy? Mother tried to talk Father into telling Grandma to leave her livestock to Hööshek since otherwise Hööshek might think they had taken in her sister only because of the livestock. Father thought otherwise: Hööshek could think what she liked, but this was about Grandma, and so whatever happened was fine as long as her feelings were not hurt.

Father and Mother turned to Grandma. She met them halfway: "You surely noticed that the words were stuck in my throat, and that I did not know how to put them. My flock is not great in numbers, but some of it came down to me from my father's flock, and the rest is the fruit of my whole life's arduous work. So I would love to leave it with all my blessings to the child who has now at the end of my life softened my liver and lit up my soul. Yet there is . . ." She fell silent. Father hastened to help her along: "Forget people's black tongue, *Awaj*. It will pale with the white of your blessing and our awe of your white head."

"You are right, Schynyk," Grandma said in her calm, steadfast way, "he who knows himself in the white need not fear the black. But I was thinking of the quota and the state law behind it. You already have enough trouble with your own livestock without adding mine to the flock and making your life even harder."

"If that is all, *Awaj*," Father said, relieved, "do what seems right. The boy will be grateful to you all his life just as I am grateful to those from whom my flock has come down to me, because it is my flock that feeds me and my children and that will continue to feed my children's children and their children."

Around the middle of the first summer month Grandma rode back to her sister's yurt. She took Molum along as a drover. Father and Mother had argued that there was no rush to get the flock and that it would be better for her to get it in the fall when the *ails* had moved closer together. And as for her clothes,

Grandma had already sewn the odd piece anyway. But Grandma thought that her animals should get used to our pasture and to the other members of their new flock before the arrival of winter, and that we should look at each animal in turn and imprint it on our memory—the earlier, the better.

Then disaster hit our *ail*, our yurt, me: I fell into the kettle, into the simmering milk.

It happened the evening Grandma rode off to get my future flock and bring it into the *hürde* for me. Mother had poured the fresh milk into the cast-iron kettle for boiling and, because the fire was burning too high, had taken the kettle off the *oshuk* and temporarily put it on the three chunks of dung lying next to it.

Then she left the yurt again to tether the calves since the yak herd had just returned from pasture. In the meantime, Father was busy outside with the lambs, along with Brother and Sister. Even though I was not yet changed and prepared for the night, I had, as often before, been overcome by tiredness, had crashed in the middle of playing, and now lay asleep on the low bed. Mother was about to sneak up and catch the last fugitive calf when she heard my screams. She became alarmed but tried to calm herself by reasoning I was crying because I had awakened afraid. Not wanting to run back to the yurt before she had caught all the calves and completed the last task of the day, she held out until she got hold of the straggler and tied it to the *dshele*. Once that was done, she raced back to the yurt as fast as she could because my screaming not only continued but was now cracking and threatening to choke me. By then the fire in the *oshuk* had gone out, leaving the yurt in darkness. Mother kindled a light and found me in the kettle, floating on top of the milk, my limbs stretched apart and stiff with fear. My head, arms, and legs were barely recognizable on the surface. But this must have saved me, otherwise I surely would have drowned. The kettle was large enough to submerge an entire wether, and that night the milk reached almost to its brim even though it was early in the year and the milking season was just beginning.

Since Grandma had moved in with us, the old practice of keeping me on the tether had become unnecessary even when I was fidgety. I had grasped that perfectly well and had in fact weaned myself, which became obvious the day after Grandma had left, when Mother tried to return me to the rope and it no longer worked: I fought against it with everything in my power, and won in the end.

Fortunately, I remember nothing about the incident. And fortunately, no one remembers the details of what happened next. Not Mother, who must have fished me out of the milk, nor Father, who must have come running when he heard the two screaming and howling voices, nor Brother or Sister, who showed up soon after but had to dash off to get the other *ail* people to help—none of them has ever been able to give me the whole story. Or maybe none has been willing to. Maybe something occurred that has remained unspeakable. The first express messenger left the *ail* right away. He took his message to the next *ail*, and from there other men rode on to other *ails*. As a result, very soon the news was flying in all directions at the speed of a horse that is whipped non-stop. It was in my favor that all this happened shortly before the National Holiday, when the race horses had already been caught and were being broken in. That night was their first and possibly hardest trial of strength because they had to run several *örtöö* under heavy saddles and heavy grown men. Their only breaks came when they reached an *ail*. Their paths led across mountains, through the steppe, and across rivers to the next *sums*, where Urianghais and Dörbets as well as Kazakhs, Torguts and other tribes lived, each with their own language and their own body of knowledge. The first of the men returned before midnight. He brought bear fat that had matured for ten years to brush on my burned skin. Others returned with fat from wild horses or wild camels, from badgers or sables, even from marmots, and again and again from bears, all well-matured, much of it almost a human lifespan old.

The older it was, the more liquid and clear the fat had become: twenty-five-year-old bear fat was like spring water. The Tuvans were accomplished hunters as well as herders, but strangely enough, very few knew that the fat of wild animals was medicinal. Whatever was brought in from the outside during those days, in exchange for horse sweat and pleas, would have been available in almost any yurt in our own *ail*. But since it was not at hand, people approached the novelty with awe, and so it came about that I was soon floating in fat. Yet nothing—nothing seemed to help. The naked creature I had become—my torso was almost completely skinned—continued to scream long after having grown hoarse and having run out of tears. I shook and trembled and showed signs of the most terrible suffering. The only skin left undamaged was toward the outer ends of my limbs, on my face, my neck, and a small area around my navel. Given the circumstances, I was lucky that my hands and feet had been spared so that people were able to stand me on my feet and hold me by my hands.

Two days later, toward evening, the last horseman returned. It was Dambi, who was related to Mother and thus a *daaj* to me. He brought something we had never seen before, something we had never even heard of: a hardened light mass that melted and liquified when it was heated. It was called *dawyyrgaj*, which meant nothing to us at the time. But later, when I was well traveled in the world of languages, I realized it was a variant of the Mongolian word for resin. The *dawyyrgaj* was the resin of a certain tree and did indeed possess magic power. Barely had it been brushed onto my skinless, greased, and shiny flesh when I, the suffering child, stopped screaming and trembling, and soon after went to sleep. I slept for a long, long time. But my sleep was arduous because it was impossible to put me into a comfortable sleeping position, and so people had to keep holding me just as they had before. A cape that surrounded both me and the person helping me to remain standing protected me from the cold and the draft and from idle glances—glances from which Tuvan children since time immemorial have been protected when they fall ill.

It was hard on whoever held me, whoever crouched in front of me and pulled me up by my wrists, always anxious not to let my slippery, limp body slide from his hands. It didn't take long for his forearms to tingle and then to burn and eventually for his arms to lose all sensation and turn numb, while helplessly he watched his charge slip from his hands, millimeter by millimeter. Then he needed to be replaced, there was no other way. Father and Mother took turns. Whoever had just been replaced had to take care of life inside the yurt. Neighbors took care of everything outside.

When I woke up, I started to scream again, but now it was different. I no longer screamed in alarm, and no longer screamed to fight for a life that was about to be cut short.

One day, a third pair of hands came to support me, Grandma's. Oh yes, Grandma: All those days and nights she had crouched in silence in front of the stove, and all day and night she had kept the fire going, which had been the only assistance she had dared, and been allowed, to provide.

She had returned the very next day after she had ridden away. By then, word of the disaster had criss-crossed the country but, strangely enough, it had not reached Grandma. She came back with all her remaining possessions. Once she was back in the yurt, she learned what had happened. Mother received her not with the joyful greeting she must have anticipated but with an admonition: "See? So that's why you were so hell-bent on taking off. It was the evil spirit that possessed your damn beasts and called for you!"

Grandma slumped, dropped to her knees, and remained crouching, mute and motionless. Only her gaze flitted about. Her eyes were dry and shiny and, in a way, spoke—screamed.

Father and Mother did suffer deeply because of my disaster. But I will never fully grasp the agony Grandma had to bear. Only a person who has suffered as much as Grandma can understand how horrific, how immeasurable and ineffable her pain was. Not only had my accident dashed, with one stroke, the joys of motherhood she had found after years of loss, but it had also made her feel guilty for having caused the suffering of others. Mother could just as well have said the opposite of what slipped from her mouth, such as: "Don't worry, *Daaj*, we had bad luck; it was nobody's fault," but not even that would have changed anything. Mother never forgave herself for having loudly and rashly accused an elder, an old person who at the end of her hard, lonely, and almost meaningless life had unexpectedly found a glimmer of hope that she might end her life among people who loved her, and that she might leave behind somebody on this earth who would remember her fondly and benefit from her efforts.

As Grandma joined in and fought against the force with which the earth pulled me toward itself, her hands fought directly for my life. While admittedly her strength could not compare with that of Father or Mother—who at that time were young, healthy people—her meager strength was out of all proportion to her will. With numb arms and a stiff body she fought against gravity, determined not to give up the fight. She had to be replaced almost by force when others noticed how terrible she looked with her clenched, toothless jaws and her convulsively trembling head. Still, it was better this way, and not only for Grandma. Otherwise she would have remained crouching in front of the stove, feeling unneeded, if not rejected, while chores piled up by the hour, only to be taken care of by Father and Mother.

Eventually, the burn healed and I survived—something I need not go into here—for which I am eternally grateful. I am grateful not only for the sake of my own small body and soul, but also for the sake of the people who suffered because of me, and above all, for the sake of Grandma and that tiny glimmer of hope she came to so late in her life.

The disaster, which had hit with lightning speed, left me with my bare life and a stark-naked body. Like a fledgling, I lived in a cage. When we moved, I stood or crouched on all fours in a softly padded basket perched high upon a camel. Next to me on a thick felt cushion sat Grandma, with her legs stretched out, keeping an eye on me. When it was cool or rainy, she covered the basket, but when it was warm and sunny, the top of the basket remained open, and Grandma chatted with me.

In this way we moved all summer up and down the mountain valleys of Borgasun and back and forth across the mountain passes. And when we crossed the five arms of our milky-white mother-river, Ak-Hem, under the autumn sun to move north again, my wound had formed a scar, and the dead skin looked like aspen bark as it began to detach from the new skin underneath. Initially, the new skin was bumpy and patchy, but with time it became smooth and strong. And as the cold weather approached, the fact that clothing arrived to cover my body meant once and for all that I was saved.

Grandma was happy in the last years of her life. We had each other, we were with each other, we lived for each other. We formed a small family within the larger one. All sorts of things happened in the large family, but in our small one, harmony reigned forever and the little sun of happiness kept shining. Grandma saw her late dreams fulfilled, lived inside some of them, and helped to shape their future course.

Grandma and I had our own space in the yurt. It was the right upper quarter. Grandmothers always seemed to live on the right side of a yurt; it was the same in other families. In other yurts, though, it was the lower quarter. And not every grandmother had a child of her own, let alone a flock she owned together with that child.

Oh yes, the flock! It was my pride and joy. All the sheep were Blackface and had stumpy ears. Of smaller build than our breeding stock, they also had a shorter fleece. Father said our own sheep belonged to a nobler breed than Grandma's. But that was much later, and his remark stung me as if he had insulted Grandma herself.

Grandma said she had brought back just twenty-one animals as some had got away in Hööshek's herd.

"What do you mean, *Daaj*? Got away?" Mother flared up. "Hööshek gave them away!" But Grandma stayed calm and explained: "Of course animals can get away. Mine drowned in the big herd and got away." Mother wanted to give Grandma a piece of her mind, but Father stepped in ahead of her: "You didn't stand next to Hööshek when she took the animals. Maybe they really did get away. You have to learn to master your mouth, woman! As the saying goes, people rarely meet with their death because of a horse but often because of a mouth."

Mother was always ready for an argument, and she was no less equipped with sayings than Father. So she countered him with another saying: "Dogs hate to see you with a cane in your hand, and people hate to hear you with the truth in your mouth!" Grandma cleared her throat, which was a sign that she too wanted to say something. So everybody waited, and the argument that had just got going came to a halt. Grandma took her time, and what she eventually said was this: "Silk is precious; wear it if you can afford it. But what if you needed a particularly useful cleaning rag and took silk instead?"

You often had to search for the meaning in Grandma's words. That seemed to be the case now. Father and Mother were silent and reflective. The conversation died down, and the argument disappeared. It had come to an end.

I learned to count the sheep. Some days I did it twice, in the morning when the flock still lay in its *hürde*, and in the evening when it returned from pasture. Grandma taught me the numbers. She had ten fingers, five on each hand. I had just as many, although mine were quite different from hers. If you added all of our fingers together plus an imaginary one, since we had no more fingers, that's how many sheep we had. Two were wethers. They were big and fat, and we called them Grandma's two thumbs. They were thought to be getting on, even though they were born more recently than Brother and Sister, who were still only children. Maybe Aunt Galdarak was right when she said: "You'll never get this world figured out!"

When an animal was getting on, it had to be slaughtered. Rather than letting it get really old and perish, it would be used to feed the people who had raised and kept it alive all its life.

It was the same for our two wethers. First the older one was slaughtered. It happened in late autumn when a number of animals were slaughtered with an eye toward winter supplies. Grandma said the two of us should be self-sufficient: Why else did we have our own flock? I repeated her words often and to many people. To prove what I was saying, I would point first to the live wether and then to the frozen block of meat made up from small animals, which was clearly the biggest block of its kind: "Those are the winter supplies for Grandma and me."

As for the other wether, I will talk about him later. So far, twenty sheep were left. Twelve of them were ewes. All of them would lamb, and all their lambs would thrive. One or two of the ewes might give birth to twins. And one or two of the ewe lambs might already lamb themselves next spring. Such things did happen, sometimes. And so I calculated. My head was full of numbers. They were good, glorious numbers because they were obedient and always ran in the same direction, just as lambs always run toward their mothers. They complemented each other and complemented our flock. For the numbers were lambs, always lambs, stumpy-eared Blackface twin lambs, yearling lambs, second-birth lambs, and even lambs received as gifts. Yes, it was not unlikely that a *daaj* or a *güüj* would give me a little lamb as a present, and so might a neighbor or a friend or . . . oh, all this, all of it, was possible because it did happen often—did it not?—that lambs were given as a gift. Sometimes only tiny little kids were given, but of course I would prefer a lamb. Other times, the gift was a little yak calf or even a foal, but I'd be happy enough with a lamb, a tiny little lamb. . . .

The numbers were elusive, sometimes worse than foals who quickly learned to evade the lasso. But I went after them, stubbornly and tirelessly, until they eventually fell into line like a herd of trained, tamed, and tired animals. I looked into the future, pushed ahead like the planners of the Party, and discovered ever more resources—I noticed in all sorts of places little lambs I might lure into my flock.

You have already heard of Grandma's gray mare; I imagined her to have offspring, too, even though she was, relatively speaking, as old as Grandma.

I raced ahead of time and was determined to have no less than forty animals in my flock by early summer of the year when my second wether was still alive.

Spring came, and the ewes lambed. But there were no twin lambs and no yearlings. Instead, I got four gift lambs, which was more than I had counted on. But they all came from the same *hürde*.

That same spring something incredible happened: The gray mare, who was no longer gray but white, foaled and had a foal as colorful as a magpie! A few days later, though, it got eaten by wolves. Neither Grandma nor I ever got to see the pretty foal. The first joyful and then sad news remained for us but a rumor, a dream with a rude awakening. Grandma calculated that the mare must have been twenty-one years old by that time. For a horse, that was a very old age indeed. And yet she would live for another two years. Which means I waited two more times, to no avail, but she never foaled again. I would have preferred to keep waiting, but Father and Mother gave me no peace.

They thought the animal might die and end up un-
clean and useless, so I let them talk me into giving her
up for slaughter. It was called something else, though:
"to fill the kettle."

By the way, I gave up my mare for free, without
exchanging her for some other animal, as I would
when one of my sheep had become too old and had to
be slaughtered or sold. During one such trade of one
sheep for another, Mother said to Father: "He'll follow
in Stalin's footsteps. You'll see!" Note that Mother was
not talking about the Georgian Dzhugashvili's son,
who had made it into the Kremlin. She meant a different one, namely the Tuvan Lobtschaa's son, who stayed
in the Altai Mountains all his seventy-seven years and
now rests in the Altai soil. He was the oldest and the
most powerful of my six *daajs* and had many distinc-
tive traits, good ones and bad, and when Mother made
that remark, I think she meant his greed. Why was I
now suddenly so generous, and with a mare at that?
Maybe because I had rarely seen the mare. She had
not found her way into my heart like the sheep, whom
I saw and counted each morning, and with whom I
lived day in and day out. Or maybe I was related to the
nitwit who trains his eye on so many crumbs that he
can't see the lump. Or maybe this mare was something
like the scaffold of my dream since she had promised
me a foal—a mount-to-be for the man-to-be—and
now that the scaffold was to be cut down and my

dream bound to fade, my pain was too great for me to think of such trifles as a replacement?

The mare was worn out. And as for the one she had served, her time was coming, too, to go and to leave to someone else the space her life had filled. But that time had not quite arrived. Grandma was still alive, and she still crouched next to me. She watched me and took delight in seeing me thrive. I asked her a thousand questions a day, and she never tired of explaining to me all the things I came across and didn't understand, just as she never tired of telling her stories. She had much to tell, had lived for a long time, and had maintained an open mind. She knew no haste and would dwell on some stories for days. If I asked, she told many of them over and over. Her memory was good, like a well-ordered bookcase. She never had to search but seemed to keep her stories handy, each bound like a book, titled, and likely numbered as well. With her, details mattered, as did every word.

Often I asked for the story of the Dökterbej Mother.

Though I found it hard to believe, it must have been true since Grandma said so: She, too, had once been a child. One day, she was herding the flock of sheep. It was early summer, and each day was longer than the one before. That particular day seemed especially long and boring to her, so she decided to visit a yurt on the other side of the steppe. She left the flock to graze and rode off. Because the distance was considerable, she rode quite hard. As she approached her destination, the yurt's dog ran out to meet her. She slowed her horse to a walk, and only then noticed that it had begun to sweat. She was horrified. What if the person who was about to step out of the yurt and restrain the dog was a grown-up? He would immediately see that a horse had been ridden into the ground when the rest period for fattening had already begun!

An old woman stepped out of the yurt. Grandma, or rather the child she then was, recognized her immediately and was even more horrified. The woman was dreaded: everybody called her the Black Hag, and some mothers used her name to scare their young children. Those who felt kindly toward the old woman called her the Dökterbej Mother. Dökterbej was her son. Most of the stories that were told about her were terrible.

The old woman was indeed very black. Her face and her hands were smeared with soot, and her clothes were jet-black.

Out of habit, the mount went up to the yurt. Had it been up to the rider, they both would have fled. But there on the yurt's sunny side the child now sat in her saddle, having ended up in front of the Black Hag, and the young Grandma was too scared even to say hello. The old woman looked at her, grimly it seemed, and said: "Your horse is sweating as if it's been ridden by the devil himself, and you're still sitting there above it as if you can't even get off by yourself—now how's that?" Her voice sounded hoarse and mocking but not, by and large, malicious.

The child dismounted, prepared for the worst. The worst were a few slaps on the bottom or somewhere on the shoulders. But nothing like that happened. Instead, she was served porridge. The porridge had sat in a wooden bowl for a while, tasted of creamy yak milk, and contained finger-thick lumps which fell apart all on their own and melted as soon as the tongue pressed them against the roof of the mouth. I had eaten porridge quite a few times myself and cream as well, with yellow butter, and once even with ground sugar. But the porridge Grandma had that day was very special, was even better. Every time I listened, the story made my mouth water. And I felt sorry for not coming earlier into this world while the old woman who was not evil and who prepared such wonderful porridge was still around. If I had, I would have gone to her yurt instead of Grandma, or better still, together with her.

One day Mother, who was also listening to the story, gave us pause to think: "But *Daaj*! In spite of it all, the Dökterbej Mother must have been a witch. People all over talk about her, and each story is scarier than the one before!"

Grandma slowly lifted her head, which she had kept bowed as she always did after finishing a story.

And with her mild eyes aimed at Mother, she said in a voice that was a bit deep for a woman's and sounded gentle, yet firm: "Have you met her?"

Mother had not met her.

"That's it," Grandma continued gravely, "you have never met her, but I have. And the woman I met was not a witch but a human being. An old woman, as my mother was and yours is, as I am now and you will be." Mother said nothing in return, and she never again interfered with the story, no matter how often it was told.

Most beautiful were the winter evenings. The stove would drone or hum, and the sound would travel and make the kettle resonate while the meat bubbled inside, and the smell would flow from the kettle and would, moment by moment, grow denser until it seemed to send out its tendrils and blend and become one with everything we could see in the flickering light. In these moments I believed I could sense life itself. The sensation was as corporeal and palpable as if I stood in a river and felt the prickling, cooling water on my skin. Grandma crouched in front of the stove door. Father worked on the remains of a yak hide, and we could hear him pant as he always did when he had to work hard. Mother busied herself with a piece of clothing. And the children were playing, throwing *gashyk*. One moment Grandma would appear in the light, only to disappear in the dark in the next. The *düüleesh* flared up quickly but burned down just as quickly, and more had to be added to the fire all the time. We were all gathered around the oil lamp, and the conversation was quiet, harmonious, unhurried. We took turns speaking. Mother and Father usually reported what had happened during the day. Grandma added explanations and time and again developed them into stories. Nobody interrupted her, nobody interrupted anybody, everybody got rid of what was on his or her mind. And nobody interrupted what they were busy doing, either.

Everybody listened to the conversation, including the children, who were throwing *gashyk* and wished for so many horses to be revealed—and who saw that so many horses were revealed—and they loved it. It felt so good to play. Yet the children never lost track of the conversation even though they would not butt in unless they were asked a question. Everybody took part in everything. Sometimes there was a longer pause, but nobody ever rushed to break it. Rather, we would let it last and muse upon it. This way everybody seemed to be getting prepared for the night's rest.

Sometimes Grandma rested. Then Sister and Brother had to take turns crouching in front of the door of the round sheet-metal stove and tending the fire. It must have been hard work since whoever was crouching there at any given moment would plead with the other that it was time to switch places. At such moments, I was an outsider. I was the lucky on-looker who was above Brother and Sister's trials but offered commentary whenever it pleased me. After all, I was not only the youngest child, I was also the scalded child. Whenever I felt like it, I would flaunt my scalding. And was I ever able to do so convincingly! Maybe Mother Nature had added a small portion of acting talent before she dropped me in solid form into life and left me to live and die. But even when we were deeply engrossed in our games, I would never forget to slip quickly over to Grandma, whether she was up or in bed, and stroke her bald head or gently pull at her ear lobes, which felt strangely cool and hung low, weighed down by the heavy silver earrings all grown-up Tuvan women wore in those days.

Grandma was always attentive. Even in her sleep her hand would reach out for me and stroke my hair or my cheeks, and whenever my head happened to get under her nose, she would sniff it and make a muffled, gurgling sound, like a sleeping mare who senses her foal close by.

Grandma stayed as old as she had been before, and just as nimble and useful. Only her eyes grew older, as you could tell when she was sewing. When she lost the needle, she had to finger the quilted mat with both hands until one of her fingertips happened across it. Mother would shake her head and say: "But *Daaj*, haven't I told you it's time you stopped sewing!"

Grandma would reply cheerfully: "It's not that I should stop—it's that my eyes should stop being so lazy. And they will, once I've rinsed them with the water of my little one."

I didn't need to be told twice. Already I stood in front of her with my pants down to my knees.

"Shall I, *Enej*?"

"Can you?"

"Oh yes."

Grandma held out her cupped hand, and I peed into it.

"Is that all?"

"For now."

"Don't stop halfway through, I've told you that's no good. But I don't need any more, a handful is plenty."

"No, *Enej*! What a waste to pee on the ground. I'd rather you have it. You must rinse your eyes carefully."

Grandma let me talk her into holding out her cupped hand a second time. Then she said: "That's enough. Let it all go."

I had nothing left anyway. It was fun. And it felt good to know that I was doing something useful for Grandma.

———

One day Grandma's teeth had grown old as well. And when they could get no older, they began to fall out. She pulled the last ones herself. She had to wrench them quite a bit. It was better, more comfortable this way, she said.

Grandma's teeth were different from ours, they were yellowed and worn at the tops but very long and strong at the roots, and seemed to be made of stone. Arsylang would not eat them. No matter how often I wrapped them in wether tail fat, he always let the tooth drop while he flattened and relished the slice of fat on his tongue before swallowing. Never before had he rejected any teeth that had been thrown to him wrapped in fat. Both Sister and Brother had lost tooth after tooth, all of which had been wrapped in a thin slice of fat and thrown to Arsylang, always with the chanted plea: "Take the old tooth, give a new one back!"

Sister and Brother actually did get all their teeth back. And I wanted desperately for Arsylang to take at least Grandma's last teeth and replace them with new ones. But he wasn't willing, and so it happened that Grandma never did get new teeth.

So I had to help her chew as well. Whenever I thought of it, I chewed pieces of dried curd cheese and filled Grandma's wooden bowl with them. And each time she would praise me: "The curd's been chewed so well again, so smooth and juicy!"

I had various dreams for the future. The most important one was a yurt of my own. I wanted to live in it with Grandma. And grazing around the yurt would be a large flock we would own together. That I would also need a wife, and have children with her, had not yet crossed my mind. Grandma was to be with me, next to me, for me—why would I need a wife?

Yet something made itself felt that made me think, or rather worry. And sure enough, one day Grandma said the time had come for her to go home.

"But you are home, Grandma!" I called out in surprise.

She smiled and thought about it. Then she said: "I have to go. Everybody has to, at some point. There is no other way." And after a pause she added: "But I will come back."

"When?"

"When you're as big as your father is now."

"But that's too long. I won't let you go, Grandma."

"All in good time. You mustn't rush me. Otherwise I might lose my way and come back to somebody else instead of you."

"But you must come back to me, Grandma. Me! I'll live in my own yurt, and the flock will have grown."

"Of course I'll come back to you, my little squirrel."

"Try not to get any older, Grandma. Otherwise, who knows, maybe you'll lose your way. And don't forget to rinse your eyes with pee more often. I hope you'll find a boy there like me who'll give you his pee. But woe betide you, Grandma, if you decide to stay with that boy for good!"

"I won't get any older. Rather, I will grow younger, ever younger and smaller, until I am a baby again. Once that has happened, I'll hasten back, back to you."

This seemed strange and frightened me: Not Grandma, but somebody else? A little baby, of all people? "But I don't want anybody else, I don't want a baby, I want you back, Grandma."

"But the other one, the baby, that will be me, darling."

"A baby—and you'll still find your way back?"

"Everybody finds his way back, so why not me as well?"

This made sense. Everybody finds his way back meant that other people, too, had to go home, hence the notion that everybody has to. It followed that I, too, would have to go one day. How terrible, but also how interesting! But I kept this thought to myself. Instead I asked Grandma how I would recognize her once she had turned into a baby.

"You just will."

She said it cheerfully and firmly.

—

The nearer Grandma got to her end, the more stories she told and the more instructive her stories became. The very last story I heard from her was this one: Grandma did not think much of superfluous habits. By that she meant smoking, taking snuff, and drinking. Yet once she had drunk a whole bowl of liquor made from fermented mare's milk, and since then she knew that sometimes the bad can be better than the good.

One day, during the foaling season, a horseman arrived at a late hour. He was a much dreaded ruffian who was now drunk to boot. Understandably, people hoped to get rid of him peacefully, and so Grandma quickly filled a huge bowl with the steaming hot liquor that had just been distilled, and offered it to the guest in response to his greeting. He took the gift from her, had a sip, paused, tasted it again, and began to roar: "Why don't you knock back this dog piss yourself, woman? Go right ahead! Or else I'll knock your brains out and tear your yurt's roof ring down onto the stove!"

That's when Grandma remembered that there had been salt in the bowl. She grabbed the brine from the roaring and raging man's hand and did as she was told. Fear was simply bigger than disgust. As a result, she became very sick, but in the end some good came of it, too: she had been suffering for some time from a stubborn case of diarrhea, which now finally seemed cured. She thought about it and decided to test the cure on an animal should she ever get the chance. Soon she got her chance, and the cure proved effective. And ever since then Grandma had known how to cure diarrhea, whether it was she herself who suffered from it or a sheep.

One day I noticed that Grandma was eating less than she used to. Her bowl was tiny as it was. But now she asked that it be filled only halfway. Was she already on her way to becoming a baby? Could she perhaps become one without having to go home first?

I lived in fear as well as in hope.

THE *AIL*

We walked back home unhurriedly. Grandma pointed to the birds clamoring and romping in the air, and the flowers piercing the ground and rising from the steppe around us in a multitude of colors like glittering splashes that had drizzled down from the sun, the sky, the glaciers, and from mountain ridges that seemed to smoke and blaze with all this light.

In front of us lay the *ail* like a well-ordered board game. The *hürde* wasn't yet black with dung or checkered white with loose wool, but stood out brownish against the green of the grass because the *ail* had moved there only two days before. The four yurts looked as if somebody had thrown *gashyk*; one stood a little to the side and seemed round and upright like a well-built and tightly hobbled horse, while the others were herded together and resembled goats. Each seemed to lack something.

One of the yurts was very small and had four sides, but was covered with snow-white canvas that sparkled in the sunlight. It belonged to Aunt Galdarak. She was the younger of Father's two sisters. Aunt Galdarak had a daughter who still lay in her cradle and had a famous name that nobody among us had ever gone by. Her name was Dolgor. For five years Aunt Galdarak had been up to mischief far off in the south. That's what Father said. Others said so, too, although they all told different stories. Aunt Galdarak had her own stories. She had seen the capital and eaten bread. She had been a soldier and played war with a wooden gun. Nobody knew what war was, but everybody agreed it was terrible. We had never played war. The grown-ups would not have allowed it anyway. There were many things they did not allow. For example, they forbade us to play wolf, or even to call its name. We said *Eshej*, "Grandpa," and knew whom we meant. "Bad games lead to bad things," Grandma said. Aunt Galdarak had played war and had bad luck as a result. The man she was married to had walked out on her in that faraway place and disappeared. Aunt Galdarak had only recently returned—with her daughter and her tiny, snow-white yurt, a yurt such as nobody in these parts had ever seen, let alone owned. It was a fancy yurt whose *dör* was decorated with a suitcase and a mirror.

The yurt next to it, which was larger but not as bright, belonged to Father's other sister. This aunt was called Buja, and her husband was called Sargaj. They had five children, each spoiled worse than the other. That's what Father and Mother said. But I envied them because, for example, they were all allowed to smoke. It often happened that Uncle Sargaj and Aunt Buja sat around the stove with their five children, all seven of them smoking. The inside of their yurt was blue with smoke and gave off the same wonderful smell as the people in the *sum* center. Each winter Aunt Buja and Uncle Sargaj's family settled in the center, and Munsuk, the youngest of their three sons, told us that while they were there, they were free of their animals from morning to night, and for months at a time.

The third yurt looked almost black, and its felted sides and roof were riddled with holes. It belonged to Uncle Sama. He was Father's only brother and was, as we later learned, ten years younger. People said Uncle Sama would always stay a child. But he was big and terribly strong. Like many children, he did not like to wash his face. (Neither, at times, did I, particularly when Father was away.) People said the same sort of thing about his wife, Aunt Pürwü. But they did not dare to say so too often, and particularly not too loudly, because she was a shaman. With shamans you had better live in friendship. That's what Mother said. And Father not only agreed but added: "Same with dogs!" But not everybody seemed to know that. Least of all Uncle Sargaj. He used to cheer on the *ail* children, and so we made fun not only of Uncle Sama but also of Aunt Pürwü. And oddly enough, the two of them often made fun of each other. We spent hours in their yurt, listening to and laughing loudly at their sparring.

Everybody in the *ail* except Grandma, Father, and Mother were people of the new era. That's what Uncle Sargaj said. He could tell because like everybody else in the new era, they all smoked. Aunt Pürwü, though, smoked only when she shamanized. Then she sat with her back to the stove in the yurt's upper right half, smoked one pipe after the other, and sang. Her songs were pleas addressed to the spirits, whom she implored to appear at long last. It sometimes took them quite a while. And when eventually the moment arrived, she rose, and the actual shamanizing that everybody had impatiently been waiting for could finally begin. Until then, she crouched with her face turned away from both the stove and the people, shook her head, and smoked and snarled. And each time a pinch of tobacco turned to ash and Aunt Pürwü exhaled, she reached back with her right hand, which held the empty pipe that was made from a wether's shoulder blade. Then the pipe lighter would take the pipe from her, refill it with tobacco, light it, and put it back into the hand that was still waiting behind her back with spread fingers. Not even Uncle Sama, whom Father called a rotten puffer, smoked as much as she did on these occasions.

Uncle Sargaj was an elegant man. He smoked a pipe while everybody else rolled little tobacco sausages with bits of newspaper. You couldn't compare his brass pipe to the shaman's, though. Mother would have also liked to be a person of the new era and smoked sometimes herself, but she had to do so secretly because Grandma and Father were not supposed to know.

The felted door of our yurt had already been rolled up onto the roof while they were still hanging down at the other yurts. None of the children from the other yurts were visible, and I knew they were still asleep. And so were Uncle Sargaj and Uncle Sama. Father grumbled: "Those going downhill have a big sleep!"

Things were indeed going downhill with them: Each of the other families was down to just one *höne* of lambs and kids, and none of these was even full, so that Aunt Galdarak's four lambs and three kids had been added. On the other hand, we had six *höne*, all with lambs. And yet at some point our grandfather had given all these siblings the same number of animals. Ours had multiplied, while theirs had dwindled.

During Aunt Galdarak's absence Uncle Sargaj and Aunt Buja had looked after her animals. Now only a tiny number remained. But neither Aunt Galdarak nor her sister or brother-in-law made a fuss about it. Times had changed, they said. The new era had begun, and you no longer needed animals. Uncle Sama and Aunt Pürwü said so, too.

"Maybe they're right after all?" Mother said one day. "Everybody is saying the same thing, and they can't all be wrong!"

"Nonsense," Father flared up. "I am somebody, too, and so are all the others, all the people who cling to the herds that have already fed our parents and our ancestors, and that will feed our children and children's children for all eternity!"

Grandma agreed with Father. "Trust your husband, Balsyng, particularly these days, when people are getting their heads turned," she said firmly.

I immediately ran over to Uncle Sama and Aunt Pürwü's yurt. The *ail* people had gathered around the kettle simmering with porridge tea. I looked carefully at people's heads, but I could not detect anything suspicious. They seemed to be right where they had always been.

Usually we finished tethering or untethering the lambs of our six *höne* before our cousins finished their single, half-full *höne*, and so we would help them fill their *höne* in the evening and empty it in the morning. "The poor pamper their children, the rich their mounts and pack animals," Grandma said. Uncle Sama and Uncle Sargaj were poor, and their children were allowed to sleep in and dodge work.

But were we rich? Were our mounts and pack animals pampered? I wasn't sure. I knew Brother and Sister were not pampered. They rose early every morning and went to bed late. They worked all day long. It was a different story with me: I was the youngest, and I was still little.

Grandma and I walked to the river, down to the shallow spot she had picked for me to wash my face and hands each morning. I stepped into the water and suddenly remembered I had forgotten to pee.

"Grandma, can I pee in the water?"

"No, darling. Haven't I told you that you must never soil a stretch of water?"

"Just this once, please?"

"No, you'd better not. If you do it once, you open the door to doing it more often. Our mother-river, Ak-Hem, will get angry."

I climbed out of the water and skipped off. I wanted to show Grandma and the mother-river that I was a good child, and so I skipped farther and farther into the steppe until Grandma called after me: "That's good enough, stay there."

Sister Torlaa and Brother Galkaan were returning from gathering dung. They walked bent over and stumbled beneath the heavy full baskets.

"Run to your brother and sister, it will give them strength," Grandma said.

As I ran toward them, I wondered how my joining them might give them strength.

"You're a strong boy!" Sister praised me when I reached them.

"Watch for any dung falling off, will you?" Brother called out.

I squeezed myself between them and watched their baskets as we walked. That not a single piece fell off annoyed me somewhat, but I was captivated by their panting.

One of Father's quirks was that he always wanted to have a big dung heap next to our yurt. No sooner had we taken the yurt parts off the pack animals' backs after a move, and he would empty the baskets and send the children out for dung.

"We won't get to finish the heap anyway, so why drive the children so hard?" Mother scolded him when again he rearmed us for yet another dung excursion. Father replied: "So what if some is left over? Others who move by will be pleased and grateful to whoever gathered it in the steppe, carried it by the sweat of his brow, and piled it up so lovingly. Why do you think we have the saying: A worthy man's yurt leaves a pile of dung behind, but an unworthy man's yurt, a pile of shit?"

Again Grandma agreed with Father, and Mother had to keep quiet. Right then, Uncle Sargaj, with his pipe already between his lips and Aunt Buja's coat around his shoulders, stepped out of his yurt. He had taken hardly ten steps when he stopped, spread his legs, and peed. While he was peeing, he kept his body straight and calm but kept turning his head. I knew he was looking at the distant mountains and the sky above. And so he did not seem to notice us as we walked past him only a lasso's length away. Brother admonished me quietly: "Don't look. One mustn't look when grown-ups relieve themselves." I tried to defend myself: "I only looked at his pipe!" But I obeyed at once and afterward only listened to the high-pitched hiss of his pee, which went on for quite some time. It always took Father a long time, too, even longer, really. But Father walked farther away, and instead of standing, he knelt. So mostly you didn't hear anything.

Grandma stood next to the dung heap and waited for us. She remarked that the baskets were full and that the pieces of dung glistened gray and were hard and dry. This was praise for Brother and Sister. I tried to draw her attention to my own contribution: "And I watched that nothing fell off, Grandma!"

"That's what I just said!" she reassured me. I could see the soft little smile in the middle of her upper lip.

And that is how our day began.

In the afternoon a *darga* appeared at the edge of the steppe. Even before they could make out his clothes, people recognized him by the way he sat on his horse. He sat across the saddle on one of his thighs. Soon they were also able to identify his clothes: the peaked cap, the high boots, and the shoulder bag, all gleaming in the sun. The chrome-leather bag at his side swung forward and backward to the rhythm of his horse's gallop, like a young black goat charging a stake and bucking.

In those days, people held *dargas* in a kind of sacred awe. All of a sudden, life in the *ail* quickened. Men hunted for their sleeves which they had taken off their coats now that it was warm again—after the cool days up in the summer camp—down in the fall camp. Women picked up pieces of clothing and whatever else was lying around—and that during the course of the day had turned into a mess—so they could put everything where it belonged or could be hidden. And the children were sent for water and dung, and reminded to blow their noses and behave themselves in front of the *darga*.

The *ail's* people and dogs all kept their eyes on the approaching *darga*. By letting his feet as well as his left fist with the reins bounce non-stop, the *darga* drove his galloping horse forward. Meant to hold the whip, his right hand, too, was clenched in a fist and resting on his thigh, a gesture that almost hid his lack of a whip and instead added to his powerful appearance. Meanwhile, the people were rushing about the *ail*, trying to hold back their dogs, while the dogs, already risen, looked back and forth from the foreign horseman to their masters, and held back.

But all of a sudden one of the dogs lost its patience. No sooner did it jerk up its muzzle, start to bark and make a quick jump, then the others joined in its barking, and all of them tore off noisily.

As the dogs charged close, the horse slowed from a gallop to a trot, and the rider slid from his thigh onto his buttocks and into the saddle where he sat still and stiff. But since his right fist remained on his thigh, he maintained at least half the look of a *darga*.

At first the dogs barked as noisily as if an enemy was approaching. While their owners shouted at them, they made a big show of jumping at the horse from all sides as if they might pull the rider from his saddle. But since they didn't follow through, their bluster became less and less convincing, and when the rider finally crossed the edge of the *hürde*, they gave up altogether and stopped in their tracks, only to walk off a little later in different directions, each eventually settling down next to its own yurt.

The *darga* steered his horse toward Uncle Sama's near-black yurt, and according to the custom of those days, he sought out the poorest people first.

Uncle Sama, the youngest son of the richest man in our corner of the world, had turned himself into one of the poorest among us, and thus endeared himself to the authorities of the day.

The *darga* never could have guessed that this supposed pillar of the people's state would only too soon become an infamous trader, and his wife a dreaded shaman. At the time, the two of them were really only just starting their careers, they still led disorderly lives, and they were poor. They had more children than lambs. These were Uncle Sargaj's words, but they were not entirely true. After all, the shortest *höne* consisted of twenty loops, while Uncle Sama and Aunt Pürwü managed no more than fifteen children in all. They had always been considered a family with lots of children, and I have a slight suspicion that the chaos reigning in their yurt made people entering it somehow more sharply aware of the large number of children inside, because it would have reminded them of a den teeming with slippery, gray pups.

Now everybody stood stunned and watched the *darga* arrive and dismount. I had already seen quite a few *dargas* and thought this one particularly elegant, young, and nice-looking. But then I got a fright, and I sensed that the fright came from outside myself, from the grown-ups. The *darga* had no lead! He was about to use the reins to tie his horse to the yurt's tensioning band. You were never allowed to do that, it was strictly forbidden! Everybody got even more frightened when Father shouted: "Hang on, boy! Hang on to the horse till I'm back!"

He meant the *darga*. The women seemed frozen. They remained bent over whatever they had been

working on while their eyes darted back and forth between Father, the head of the *ail*, and the *darga*, whom
he had just called a boy. In the meantime, Uncle Sama,
who, squatting on all fours, had stuck his head out the
door to watch the *darga* come closer, crawled across
the threshold and was now crouching outside with
a tattered *dshargak* around his shoulders and an am-
biguous smile on his face. His squinting, narrow eyes
seemed to glance in all directions at once.

The children stood with open mouths and droop-
ing shoulders, staring at the grown-ups, with little understanding of the events that were unfolding. By then
Father was returning with a leather lead, one of the
leads he had cut from the skin of the yak cow Saasgan
Ala and tanned and softened during winter evenings.
It was kept together with the other leads, the lasso
ropes, and the three-legged stools in the buckskin bag
beneath the two chests in the *dör*. Measured against
the span of Father's arms, the lead was one and a half
fathoms long, felt velvety and always warm, and shone
with a yellow glow.

This lead Father now wanted to give *him* as a present! We knew as much even before Father reached
the guest with his leadless bridle and before anything
was said. It was another one of Father's quirks that he
gave away pieces of leather he had dressed himself.
The *darga* greeted Father curtly and in Mongolian, and
got a reply in the same manner and language. But then

he had to listen to Father lecture him with a story in Tuvan. We learned only years later why that happened and what it was all about, but its gist shall be offered here ahead of time.

The *darga* was not really a *darga* at all but rather a teacher. He was called Düktügbej, and was the son of Dandisch from the Hara-Sojan tribe. Once when Father was young, he and his herd of horses tried to escape from a snowfall which over the course of several days buried much of their pasture lands. At the end of their flight he found himself on the land of the Hara-Sojan people, whose herders did not—as he had feared they would—drive him away with his starving and exhausted herd, but instead gave him a friendly welcome and invited him to stay as long as his own pasture remained under snow. And the eldest of these friendly herders was Dandisch. Father would later seek his company whenever he got a chance. He stayed overnight in his yurt, drank from the same pot of tea and ate from the same kettle of meat as his family, and carried Dandisch's children on his back and sometimes even let them ride his own horse. And Düktügbej was the oldest of Dandisch's children.

Blushing, Düktügbej now listened to the story and watched Father take the reins from his hands, swing them over the pommel, and tie one end of the lead to the snaffle ring and the other to the band around the yurt.

That done, Father led the teacher into the yurt as if the head of the yurt, Uncle Sama, was not at home. Uncle Sama himself still crouched where he had earlier made himself comfortable, still in his tattered *dshargak* and now again on all fours like a child or a dog. He viewed the guest from bottom to top with tiny, sly-slanting eyes that were narrowed to two lines, and with an idiotic and yet cunning smile on his face that was also marked with two brown trails of sweat.

The teacher greeted him immediately in Tuvan, but the uncle replied in Mongolian, or at least in something meant to be Mongolian, and pulled the same face he pulled when he tried to draw his wife into a new round of fighting.

The children learned only later what happened next. No matter how long we lurked around the yurt and how often we slipped past its open door, we had to content ourselves with unintelligible shreds of the conversation carried on inside. It was an exciting conversation, though. The names of children from our *ail* popped up again and again, which naturally increased our curiosity and desire. How could anybody think of play, let alone of the calves that had to be herded? But sadly, sadly, the guest whom we still believed to be a *darga*—which is why our noses were so clean that even Marshal Choibalsan could have inspected them—spilled over into Mongolian whenever he raised his voice.

As we would later learn, he was actually a public school teacher in the process of recruiting children for his school. In the chrome-leather bag that he carried on a shining strap over his shoulders and that dangled next to his right thigh, he carried the names of all Tuvan children who the *dargas* at the *sum* center guessed might have turned eight.

Among them were six names from our *ail*, three of whom were children of Sama's: Marshaa, Dshanik, and Tögerik. The first two were grown up: Somebody had courted Marshaa as a bride for his son, and Dshanik, the future *sum* elephant, had long ago joined the men who loaded the oxen whenever we moved. Until a year before, though, both had been considered seven-year olds, along with their younger sister, who actually might have been seven. And so it was entirely understandable that all three of them were now summoned to start school together. But Uncle Sama promptly declared the bride and the wrestler altogether too old for school, while his third child again stayed seven. Try as he might, the teacher had no luck.

The next two children in question—the girl Gökbasch and the boy Sambyy—belonged to Aunt Buja. Their father, Uncle Sargaj, had by now already twice greeted the man with the shoulder bag as a representative of the state, first in front of his own yurt and then inside Uncle Sama's yurt, where both times he had stood to attention and had bowed deeply, demonstrating his reverence with broken Mongolian and repeated offerings of his lit brass pipe. He now eagerly agreed to all the teacher's requests.

"Of course both children will attend school," he said, nodding constantly.

"But last time when the *sum* representative and teacher was here, you were just as agreeable, weren't you?" asked our visitor, the man who this year himself embodied the two roles he had just named.

"But, Comrade *Sum* Representative and Teacher, I did send the boy, Comrade Sambyy, to school."

"But, Comrade Sargaj, you did not send the girl, Comrade Gökbasch, to school."

"That's right, Comrade *Sum* Representative and Teacher. But that was last year. At that time, Comrade, the revolutionary spirit of the *arate*, of whom I am one, was not as high as it is now. It has since grown tremendously. It says so in the paper. I have heard it read with my own ears, Comrade *Darga Sum* Representative and Teacher."

"All right then. I trust you, Comrade *Arate*. Also, I understand there has been word that you want to join the Party?"

"That's right, Comrade *Darga Sum* Representative and Teacher. As surely as I am an uneducated *arate*, I feel a revolutionary heart glow and beat inside me. And I do not have the slightest doubt that the great wise Father Comrade Marshal Choibalsan and his faithful sons and students, the comrades *dargas* at the *sum*, will recognize this honest wish of the simple *arate* that I am."

In this way the dialogue between the *sum* representative and the *arate* took its course. Then the teacher turned to Father: "Your daughter—."

Father rushed to accommodate him: "Yes, daughter Torlaa is eight years old, that's right. And she, too, will attend school on the assigned date."

"Why don't you follow your older brother's example, Comrade?" the delighted teacher turned to Uncle Sama.

Uncle Sama, however, had only a small, unequivocal smile for such a comment. And even Uncle Sargaj, the glowing Party candidate, rewarded Father, his brother-in-law, with a mere smile for his forthright words.

Sobered, the teacher looked at the group and turned again to Father: "So far I've only got half of the six children from your *ail* that are supposed to go to school. If only I had four! Tell me, Uncle, what shall I do? What shall I tell the *dargas* when I get back?"

"You need one more, don't you?" Father asked instead of answering him.

"I do. At least one."

"Then take my boy as well."

"But, Uncle?!"

"He is only seven. But what's a year? It doesn't matter if he goes this year or next."

Mother, who had already flinched, only now got a chance to call out: "You want to give Galkaan away as well? You can't do that!"

"You keep quiet!" Father snapped and ordered the Dandisch son: "Write down his name. He is called Galkaan, Galkaan of Schynykbaj."

Then Father got up and left the yurt. The teacher got up as well.

When he left the *ail*, he left behind a fight. On the one side stood Father, alone; on the other side, all the *ail's* other grown-ups came together.

Grandma was still deep in thought, as one could tell by looking at her. It was not until everybody prepared for the night that she finally spoke up. "You should have talked this over with your wife first, Schynyk," she said, and in the same breath turned to Mother, who had started to look around triumphantly upon hearing these words: "And as for you, Balsyng, you need to understand that it will be easier for your daughter if she knows her brother is close by. And remember, earlier is always better than later. Your husband has surely thought of such things."

But earlier, before it came to this, everybody had spoken up against Father—and it goes without saying—behind his back. Uncle Sama called his older brother an old man whom age had made childish. Aunt Pürwü spoke of a difficult spring ahead, one that would demand great sacrifices, especially in places where many people gathered. Aunt Galdarak thought that a child of seven was not capable of learning and would die from homesickness. Even among the Khalkh people, who certainly were smarter and more courageous than us, children started school only when they were eight.

Uncle Sargaj called Father, his wife's older brother, a man who did not know how to live in the new era. He said the new era no longer called for things, but for the spirit. Words were more important than actions. Aunt Buja thought what everybody else was thinking, and what they said was fine with her; she was without a mind of her own. She simply carried words from one person to the next where they arrived as warm as the mouth they had come from. And what she carried in her mouth that day was directed against her older brother, of whom she was normally more afraid than is a child of its father.

Swarms of children gathered all over. Their conversation revolved around the leadless rider who, though not a *darga*, had been just about as elegant and as powerful as if he had been one. And since the rider was a teacher, they also talked about school and about what lay ahead for Brother and Sister, and for Gökbasch and Sambyy.

"They will go to school!" everybody repeated in shock, although nobody could imagine what it meant. The four children concerned were looked upon with both envy and pity. Each reacted differently. Sister

Torlaa was neither able nor willing to hide her joy, and trumpeted: "I'll become a teacher! But you, if you stay out here in the country without school, you will herd sheep and gather dung until you die."

Brother Galkaan said nothing. Withdrawn into himself, he looked on silently. Nobody could tell what was hidden behind his silence. But I have known him almost better than I have known myself and believe to this day that he was not thinking anything and did not care what would happen.

Cousin Sambyy, on the other hand, had already attended school the previous year and bragged: "You think you can scare me with school? Forget about it. School's great. You don't have to herd sheep or gather dung, and the way they put you up is so neat too— when you crap, you squat on two planks. Learning is no big deal. What stays in your head stays; what doesn't, doesn't. You simply prove to the teacher you're too dumb for school. If you can manage that, you'll graduate after four years."

Cousin Gökbasch did not want to hear about school. "You'll see!" she said, her lips pressed together. "I simply won't go. I'll say I have the freedom, everybody's got the freedom, it's the new era. The era of *Pidilism* is over. People can no longer be forced to do what they don't want to do."

Gökbasch kept her word. Instead of being forced to go to school, she married and did so of her own free will. The groom was a *darga* from the *aimag*. He did not speak Tuvan, and she had not mastered Mongolian. But she wanted to learn his language, and she succeeded because she lived with her *darga* in the *aimag* center. Sometimes gifts arrived from her, sweets, but not just lumps of sugar, oh no, they were fragrant, colorful candies wrapped in crackling paper, always two of them. Did the dear cousin, the elegant *darga* wife in the *aimag*, remember me? Or was it really Aunt Buja, who must have had a guilty conscience toward her brother? But the story ended badly for the one who had risen to be a *darga* wife. She died giving birth to her first child.

Uncle Sargaj, too, never had a chance to enjoy fully the fruits of the new era that pleased him so much. He died the following winter from appendicitis.

From that day onward, all the *ail's* hustle and bustle changed. The relatives avoided our yurt. Out in the *hürde*, there were no longer any intimate conversations between Mother and the aunts, nor the peals of laughter that used to accompany them. Uncle Sargaj's and Uncle Sama's remarks got more pointed. They stung Father and the children alike—even me. For example: "Hey, little one! D'you want to claw your way up to a salary, too?" I had no idea what a salary was or what it had to do with me, but I felt the scorn in the remark.

I asked Grandma. She explained: They were referring to the money that in the old days the prince and his officials, and that in the new era the *dargas* and the teachers, received from the state. To me, that didn't seem bad at all. Money, the colorful square pieces of paper, represented something valuable. I had noticed how carefully Father handled the pieces, and with how much respect Mother looked at them—I could even sense her desire at least once to hold them in her own hands. But Father did not let her have any, he never let them out of his hands.

I had also heard that you could exchange money for anything. In our family, we were short of money. We only had it in the spring, after Father took away the flocks of sheep and herds of yaks. People said they ended up at the Russian border and got slaughtered by the Russians. Maybe that is why people insulted animals by saying, "Up the Red Russian ass!" The pieces of paper one got for a boisterous flock of sheep or herd of yaks did not even fill a hand, and one by one turned into flour, rice, salt, tea bricks, candles, lead, gun powder, primer, and other stuff. And when no paper money was left but more stuff was needed, Father sold another sheep or yak cow. The Kazakhs would buy them. The Kazakhs had money. They cut down the larch forests, built rafts to take away the logs, and exchanged them in the *aimag* for pieces of paper. No Tuvan ever touched a larch with an axe or a saw unless it had fallen already. But the Kazakhs sawed or cut them down wherever they found them.

What if I had a salary? What if I owned many colorful pieces of paper? I would be so happy. I would give
them all to the grown-ups, and especially to Mother
so that she, too, could hold them in her hands and exchange them for something she would like to have. I
would also give some to Father so that he would never
again need to deliver flocks or herds for slaughter to
the Russians, nor offer any more sheep or yaks to the
Kazakhs in exchange for one or two, or more perhaps,
of the colorful pieces of paper.

The bickering in the *ail* was getting worse. It was
worst among the children when we tethered or unteth-
ered the lambs and kids.

Brother, Sister, and I stopped helping the children
of our relatives when they, as usual, could not even
manage their single *höne*. It upset them, and they
teased us. Torlaa, the devil, knew how to reply to an
angry word with an even angrier one. The sparring got
fiercer by the day.

Aunt Buja had sharp ears. Even before, she often meddled when we played, but now she was even
keener to butt in when we wrangled.

"*Kulaks!*" she railed one day. This was not the first
time we had heard the insult. Anytime someone had
something against us, he or she would say or even
yell the word. And nobody who did so ever got a reply: Neither Father nor Mother nor Grandma could
afford to reply. But this was no way to tangle with

Sister Torlaa—whose name meant "Little Partridge" but who certainly wasn't one, didn't know how to hold back, and who now flared up: "There has never been more than one *kulak* around here, and he's dead as far as I know." She meant Aunt Buja's own father, who had been the richest man in our corner of the world. She kept going: "Don't speak of *kulaks* who no longer exist. Speak of the *dshelbege* the place is teeming with!"

Aunt Buja was not prepared for this, and she squealed like a stuck pig: "You don't mean *us*, do you?"

Sister Torlaa should have been called *Mys*, "Scratching Kitten." She hissed: "Who else? How dare you claim not to be one? You have devoured your dowry and your father's wealth like a *dshelbege*. And now you're so ashamed and envious that you spit venom at whoever hasn't done the same!"

Aunt Buja jumped up, let out a scream, and ran toward our yurt, screaming loudly all the way: "Your Torlaa, your daughter, has insulted me! I'll take you to court. To court! Aaaah! Ihii-ih!" But just when she had almost reached the yurt, she turned around even while she continued screeching.

Brother Galkaan said to Sister Torlaa: "Watch it. Mother's going to give you a thrashing, and maybe Father will as well." There was pity in his voice.

Sister Torlaa, however, raged: "So what? I've got to be able to say, to my last breath, what sounds right to me."

The aunt seemed to calm down once she had run a circle around the *hürde*. Sister remained unscathed but was admonished: "It's not right for children to argue with grown-ups."

The aunts, who used to drop by several times a day to chat and drink tea with Mother, stopped coming to our door. Instead, they now visited each other more often and drank their tea in either of their yurts, laughing especially loudly. And when they weren't taking a nap, the uncles would sneak after them and join them for the chats and the tea. When we happened to show up, we noticed them either change topics or else make sure we would not understand. But we understood plenty.

While this was going on in the other yurts, the opposite conversation was taking its course in our own. Mother held forth, and Grandma threw in her bit.

Mother called the relatives nitwits whose heads had been turned. Grandma shook her head as she listened and spoke of times that would change and diseases that would heal.

Father had no time for such talk. If he happened to catch the tail end of one of these conversations, he had nothing but disdain to spare: "Without livestock, without meat or milk—what are these purultarens going to live on? Their jabber perhaps?"

Purultarens—this was one of the fashionable words Uncle Sargaj and Uncle Sama had recently taken to. They called themselves purultarens, by which they meant proletarians. Then we heard that Uncle Sargaj was going to move and settle in the *sum* center because his children would be attending school. Reputedly Sambyy, who had spent his first year in boarding school, had become homesick and now said that he would only return if his parents moved to the center with him. And maybe Gökbasch could still be talked into going to school if her parents' yurt were next door and she knew she could go home whenever she felt like it.

So one morning Uncle Sargaj showed up with four camels he had borrowed from the Kazakhs in exchange for a ewe lamb, and the yurt was loaded up. Aunt Buja and Munsuk, the youngest of the children, sat on the white horse that always stood saddled from morning to night. Everybody else followed the packed camels on foot.

The family left their livestock to Uncle Sama. "That's madness. They will drink milkless tea as early as the hot autumn. Ask them if they don't want to take the black horse so at least they can ride?" Mother asked Father.

But Father laughed scornfully: "He who thirsts for poverty shall enjoy it to the fullest."

Until this episode, it had been customary for families who were about to move, to invite everybody who would stay behind for tea on the day before their move. And then they in turn would be invited back for early tea on the day of their departure.

But now none of this happened with Uncle Sargaj. "What strange times these are," Grandma commented.

A little later, we heard that Uncle Sama and Aunt Galdarak, too, would move to the *sum* and settle down. But they would not move until the onset of winter, and so their yurts still stood where they used to be. Having heard of the plan, Father called over to Uncle Sama, who was lying in front of his yurt tanning himself: "And what will come of your animals?"

"I'll pay the Kazakhs to look after them," was the answer that came back. Father grabbed the dog's bowl at his feet and hurled it away. The aspen-wood bowl flew across the *dshele*, across the pile of ashes, and broke in two as it landed. Brother Galkaan brought it back, and we saw that it had cracked through the middle. Father didn't have time to glue it back together. He leapt into the saddle on the black horse and trotted away with a suddenness that shocked us. Had we done the same, we surely would have been rebuked.

Father truly did not have much time to spare in those days, as we had to prepare for winter. He had only just mucked out the *hürde*, taken the dung to the winter camp, and carefully stacked the cowpats as fuel for the winter. Now he made hay on Sara Ortuluk, an island at the meeting of the two big rivers. In the morning he rode off before sunrise, and in the evening he came home after sunset. One day he took Brother and Sister along to help him gather up the hay. My job was to stay home and look after the lambs and calves. I did as I'd been told and ended up without a moment's peace all day.

Grandma and Mother had their hands full as well. They had been sewing school clothes for Brother and Sister, a quilted coat and a long winter robe for each. Each also got a bag—yes, yes indeed, a shoulder bag like the *darga's*, although theirs were made from cloth and had a red five-pointed star at the center of the top facing out. Sister Torlaa's things were all green, while Brother Galkaan's were blue. That is what the school uniform of the day was like. Finally, they both got their boots resoled, and even their felt insoles replaced.

The hay gatherers did not return until darkness had fallen. Brother and Sister were euphoric and talked of many beautiful things. I had nothing new to report. My day without them had been long. The next day Father, too, stayed home and beat a couple of sheep skins. He beat them until the compressed wool flew apart and sprung up again like the wool of an animal just slaughtered. Then he rolled up the skins and packed them into the travel bag, to which the two felt *tons*, the two school bags, and the spare underwear were later added.

That day was Brother and Sister's last day in the *ail*. Things happened that I had never seen before: Father sawed a comb out of a billy-goat's horn. Sister Torlaa was to use it to comb the shock of hair that covered her parting and hung down over her forehead. Then he carved two little sticks from willow wood, hollowed them out with a piece of red-hot wire, and poured molten lead into the holes. This is how pencils were made.

The next morning was strange. A feeling crept upon me that with each new piece of clothing they slipped into, Brother and Sister increasingly stopped being who they had been for me until then. Finally both of them stood, cowed dumb, in their new clothes in front of the grown-ups. The relatives had gathered in front of our yurt to sniff and kiss the children before they left.

They sat together on one horse, Sister Torlaa in the saddle and Brother Galkaan behind her on the bag with the sheep skins and *tons*. They sat speechless and acquiescent; their horse would follow an outrider.

The crowd of children rode alongside the departing riders as they headed toward the ford. Brother Galkaan, who had remained silent all this time, staring at his sister's back in embarrassment, suddenly called out: "Dshurukuwaa, go home!"

We had not yet reached the ford, but I obeyed and stopped. The other children galloped on, not wanting to turn back until they got to the river. When they finally came back, I had long been making my way home. They caught up with me, and I let them pass.

That morning, rain came down from the mountains in the north. It lashed the yurts, the meadows, and the river, and then left as hastily as it had arrived. Immediately afterward the sun came out, and the day turned out warm and long. That autumn was mild and lasted a long time. Much happened. But to me, the warm, long, eventful autumn seemed to be all in vain and to waste itself to no avail.

FAREWELL

Finally winter arrived. I was glad that it did and that our yurt could be moved back into its comfortable solitude. Maybe I was also glad because lately everybody had been telling me that I was a big boy and that the time had come to show whether I could guard my flock by myself.

Sure, I thought when they told me, sure I can guard my flock and look after Grandma. But I would need a yurt of my own, a big white yurt with many pretty furnishings — a palace yurt!

The *hendshe* fell to me. It consisted of lambs born late in the year or out of season, and of grown animals that, for one reason or another, could not follow the big flock to the distant pasture.

In the mornings, when the big flock had left the *hürde* and disappeared from sight, I drove my own flock to its pasture. The big flock always went uphill to the mountain ridge, whereas the *hendshe* went downhill to the mountain folds that were sheltered from the wind. But first, half the flock had to be untied from the *höne*, and the lambs and kids led out of the yurt one by one so they would not run around inside and perhaps cause damage. For the flock's other half all I had to do was open the door of the small wooden shed and the young animals inside, which were not tethered, came out on their own.

The days of winter, which seemed so short to the adults, seemed long, infinitely long to me. I was not to play but rather to take the flock to its pasture, and I was told to watch the wind, the sun, and the grass, to watch how the animals reacted to them, and to watch how each of the animals behaved. It was also important to be on my guard against wolves and eagles. Should any appear, I was told not to be afraid and to grab quickly my shepherd's crook, which I carried over my shoulder like a gun; I was to aim it at them, produce a bang, and scream loudly.

But the days of winter were not only long. More than anything, they were cold. My face and hands got particularly cold. It was strange, but people in the mountains did not wear gloves: gloves did not exist. Instead, our sleeves were long, and anything sharp-edged, cold, or hot, anything we could not touch with our bare hands, we grabbed through these long sleeves. Only toys—stones covered with hoarfrost—were to be fingered by your bare hand and touched by your skin so they could come alive and change into people and animals, into yurt utensils and other such things.

As a result my hands got cold. But what did it matter? Rather, I assured myself once again of how much I had at my fingertips and of how pleasant my life was. And besides, I had my glow stone, which I carried in my breast pocket like a little stove, a tiny sun, and which my freezing hand could touch and warm itself on any time. My right hand often reached into my breast pocket, warmed itself on the glow stone, and passed on the warmth to my left hand and my face.

The stone was the size and shape of a horse dropping, was smooth and purplish-black, and every morning was heated in the embers. It retained the heat for a long time, and when I arrived back home in the evening and took the stone from my pocket to put it aside, it still felt lukewarm.

Every morning my dog Arsylang welcomed me when I stepped out into the world. Compared to me, the world was incomparably awesome as it lay in front of me in all its mystery. And every evening it was Arsylang, again, who brought me back safely from the world of mysteries and dangers to the shelter of my parents' yurt. In the mornings, we had to hurry ahead of the flock, and in the evenings, follow behind. That was the number one rule for anybody who was willing to take upon himself the dangers lying in wait for his flock. But Arsylang always watched out for me: In the mornings, he ran out ahead of me and in the evenings, he trailed along behind me.

During the day, he crouched next to me and watched me play. I wanted him to join in, but smart as he was, he did not grasp that the sheep and goats had to be kept apart from the yaks and horses, or that the yurt had to be round and the stove at its center. From time to time I chided him, sometimes even shoved his neck, but then consoled him when I thought I detected in his greenish-brown eyes something like traces of guilt and of helpless sadness. Then I would stop playing the solitary game and play other games with him, games that he, too, was able to play: We skipped and ran, wrestled and rolled around in the snow. I was always the first to get tired and when I did, we would give up on that game as well and instead busy ourselves with the flock. Arsylang was quick, was sharpness itself, and skilled in guiding the flock. Sometimes he would punish a kid that had climbed on rocks or got up to some other silliness instead of eating its fill. His punishments varied. At best, the offender was given a little fright. At worst, he would chase an animal until it collapsed. But he inflicted the harsh punishment only when I wanted him to, and I swear that Arsylang's teeth never broke the skin of any animal in the flock.

On windless Sundays we hiked up to the top of Doora Hara. From there everything was visible as if in the palm of my hand: The big rivers that were now covered with ice and snow and were glinting in places; the *ails* along the bank on this side of the Ak-Hem; Tewe-Mojun, the Camel's Neck, and Saryg-Höl, the Yellow Lake, both brought into being by Sardakpan, the giant hero and creator of the Altai Mountains; the six Kazakh yurts that lay in regular intervals along the Homdu's left bank and almost always gave off clouds of thick smoke; beyond Ak-Hem and on the Homdu's right bank the center of the Ak-Hem *sum*, which was Kazakh; the bushes starting at Dshedi-Geshig and stretching along the Homdu until they disappeared in the ravine between the mountain ridges of Ortaa-Syn and Borgasun; the center of Tsengel *sum*, which was Tuvan; and finally the mountains in the distance, above all Harlyg Haarakan, the vast blue-white, snow-covered peak.

I had been to fewer than half of these places, but I knew all of them by name, and I knew pretty much where things were and who lived where. I knew because Grandma had a good memory and, unlike Mother, the patience to answer all my questions.

The *sum*, which always meant the center of the Tuvan *sum*, was closest to my heart. I stared at it more often and longer than at anything else, until I was able to distinguish one house from the next and thought I could even count the yurts scattered around the houses like a shooed herd. They stood out against the brown steppe, shimmering from afar. Sometimes I saw a car drive past. It dragged along a white thread of dust, which would often grow into a cloud. At other times the thread would break off and balloon into a veil of fog that grew bigger and paler until I could no longer see it.

Uncomprehending, but curious, I watched and drew Arsylang's attention to what went on beyond the two rivers and the steppe. He would stare across, prick up his ears, and growl at moving cars. And naturally, as we kept watching, I thought of Brother and Sister and discussed them with my four-legged companion. Whenever he heard their names, Arsylang became restless and whimpered. But if his whimper began to turn into a howl, I jumped in to interrupt and tell him that howling and crying might harm Brother and Sister and thus were not allowed. Then Arsylang obeyed, fell silent, and looked at me with his submissive, pleading eyes. Once, though, I did not interrupt his whimpering—I was unable because I had burst into tears myself. Arsylang immediately joined in with his muffled howling, which in turn only made me cry harder with streams of tears and noisy sobbing. And as happened so often in those days, I could not help but think about why Brother and Sister had to leave home, and for the first time ever I felt hurt by Father, who had wanted it all to be this way.

Father idolized his own father, who had been a *baj* and in some people's eyes even a *kulak*. However, Father called him something different when he wanted to call him anything besides "Father": a man with a heart for his animals. That name applied to Father himself as well.

What may have moved Father, a man with a heart for his animals, to separate his children from his animals, from the proven roots and sustenance of their lives, just when they had turned old enough to take on some of his tasks and to ease his burden? Was it the salary? People talked about the salary as if it were a little fairy-tale pot that cooked porridge whenever you asked. Or was it rather obedience to the powers-that-be, which supposedly represented the people and certainly were strict? Or perhaps a kind of trust in those powers? Or was it the perceptiveness of the *arate*, that natural ally of the victorious working class, a class which couldn't possibly have existed from the start?

I felt guilty after I had cried and I still felt guilty when I woke up the next morning. I had had a dream, and although I could not remember the details, I sensed it had been about Brother and Sister, and I felt something heavy inside me. And then Arsylang, too, seemed to go quiet and move with heaviness. Maybe my mood was indeed affecting him?

A few days went by before word arrived that flu had broken out in the *sum*. Father and Mother turned mute with fear. Their prayers, those conversations with oneself that were addressed to the mountains, the waters, and the clouds, became longer and more fervent by the day, and whereas at other times they might have taken place out of habit, as a kind of duty, they now arose from a heartfelt need. Re-awoken, my guilty conscience did not pass but gnawed at me and made my wound spread further with each passing day.

I begged the mountains, the steppe, and the sky to protect Brother and Sister from vicious and rabid dogs, from illness, and from black or white tongues. That such dangers existed I learned from the grownups as I listened to their prayers. But there were some additional pleas that I had not heard from anybody but that I came up with myself. For example, I asked of Eser-Haja, the mountain saddle, that Brother and Sister not only return happy and healthy, but also with candies. And I pleaded with the ravine below our camp and with the river that snaked through it and was now frozen stiff and seemed to be resting, to protect me from school and to let me live with Grandma and our shared flock. Because I saw that the sides of the ravine were steeper than any other I had ever seen, and because I knew that its river gathered the waters of all other rivers, I did not doubt their omnipotence.

My wishes were insatiable, my pleas unbridled. Arsylang crouched next to me and listened patiently—full of understanding, I thought—when, my arms stretched out and my head held high, I adopted the pose of an epic hero and with my high voice loudly recited my pleas.

I begged Harlyg Haarakan for a flock of a thousand. They would all be stumpy-eared Blackface, the whole one thousand of them.

"One thousand sheep—do you know how many that is?" I turned to Arsylang. "That's all the fingers of one hundred people taken together!" Arsylang tilted his head and looked at me attentively. "One hundred is a big number, too," I went on to tell my companion. "Where will we get so many people, hey?"

Arsylang realized he had been asked but could not grasp, let alone answer, the question. There was confusion in his eyes. "Never mind," I consoled him and continued: "It's winter now, so we won't be able to gather so many people. But in the summer we will. In the morning and in the evening, there will be lots of people at the dairy plant to drop off the milk. And if they don't add up to a hundred, we'll get a man to ride from *ail* to *ail* and ask that everybody quickly come to the dairy plant. People will want to know if there's a meeting."

Nobody liked to go to meetings. What people liked

to go to were feasts. So why would anybody go to the dairy plant? The messenger, before riding on to the next *ail*, would announce: "Schynykbaj's youngest, Dshurukuwaa, along with his dog Arsylang, wants to become the owner of a flock of one thousand sheep, but first he wants to see what 'one thousand' looks like by counting your fingers!"

I thought I detected a smile on Arsylang's face. It was going to be fun with all the people and their fingers. Amyj, whom Father and Mother called Uncle and whom the children called Grandfather, would exclaim: "Good Heavens! Isn't that something? So young, and already he can count to a thousand!" Aunt Tuudang, his wife, would answer: "How could it be otherwise? He is, after all, Schynykbaj's son and Hylbang's grandson." They would probably say more, but what mattered was that they, too, were going to be there, and that everybody contributed his or her ten fingers. Yet it was not so simple with everybody else. I would have to watch out for Gokasch and Dupaj: If Gokasch were there, I would have a thousand and one, but if Dupaj were included, it would be nine hundred and ninety-nine. And if both of them were among the hundred people, I would have exactly one thousand fingers. This was because Gokasch had six fingers on his left hand, while Dupaj had only four on his right. Supposedly, the former had been born this way and the latter's index finger had been torn off when he threw a lasso.

All the other people had ten fingers on their two hands. Grandma said so, and I had learned so myself. One thousand fingers all in one place? It had probably never happened. Was I the first one to come up with a plan nobody had ever been able to think of? Maybe. And that's why I could spare no effort to bring together those one thousand fingers. There would be fingers big and small, clean and dirty. Some would come with clipped nails, others with claws. Father could not stand dirty fingernails, so he would not want to help me.

Oh well, if need be we could also include the toes, which were called foot fingers in our language anyway. Instead of a hundred, we would need just fifty people. But would I be able to talk all of them into taking off their boots? Wouldn't the women who had older and highly respected male in-laws among the crowd rather die than undress their legs and show a bit of naked skin? Others, too, might rather keep their boots on than let me see their toes long enough to count them. Aunt Aewildek would call out: "Hang on, little one! My feet are dirty." And although he used to go barefoot from early summer to late autumn, Uncle Dar would probably hide his feet under his coat seam rather than let me count his toes. "My feet are nobody else's business," he would mutter. And Mother would add, "Yes, leave his out." His feet were hairy right down to their toes, and hairy feet made Mother sick, just as mice and spiders did. But then I would say that all I needed was the number of his toes, and that nothing else would tickle my nose, as Aunt Galdarak used to put it. How his toes looked and which way they went meant nothing to me.

One thousand! Oh mighty number! From one thousand pieces of livestock upward you were considered a *baj*. Grandfather had been one. Father was not. Nor was Stalin, even though he was a powerful man. "The days of *bajs* are over," Father said, "today you can work yourself to the bone and still not make it to a thousand."

Why would he say that? And why had he given away Brother and Sister?

Such were my dreams. They included the yurt Grandma and I would live in and the flock that would feed us both.

I dreamed up still more things. First, a hunting gun like the one Uncle Sargaj had: it took five cartridges, fired them in one burst, thundered loudly, and always hit its target. And a tobacco pipe like the one Galdar-Eewi's son had. One day he let me smoke tobacco in his pipe. To smoke real tobacco in a real pipe was entirely different from what we did outside with rabbit dung and the pipe we carved from a wether's shoulder bone. One puff and I was dizzy! That's when I decided: When I grow up, I want to have a pipe like that. Apparently, the older you got, the more things you had to have.

And the yurt Grandma and I would share would be big and bright. Better still, inside there wouldn't be just the two chests of drawers that belonged to any decent yurt but also the suitcase and mirror from Aunt Galdarak's yurt. But most importantly, the flock would have to be big. I wanted it to be one thousand and one animals rather than nine hundred and ninety-nine, even though I did not want to become a *baj*.

Or maybe I should? The question was directed at Arsylang. He seemed to consider it and then suddenly to nod. I was thrilled to be someone other people could not be. If I were to become a *baj* among the people, Arsylang might become one among the dogs. I asked him if he would become one. He wagged his tail. On the other hand, Father always said . . . well, if Father said so, it had to be true. But then why did everybody else talk about *bajs*? And why did Father say they no longer existed?

Arsylang barked. I looked where he looked, and caught sight of the danger. Gliding, an eagle slowly circled above the flock. We moved closer to the lambs and the kids. Born in the fall after their mothers had already had offspring in the spring, they searched for blades of grass, unaware of the threat.

"On guard, Arsylang!" I called, holding my crook in my arm like a gun. The eagle circled above us. Seemingly lifeless, it glided in an invisible orbit, descending toward us only to rise again into the sky when I screamed and Arsylang barked. Eventually it seemed to get fed up with the unsuccessful game, left us alone, and disappeared.

This way we guarded the flock and were guarded in turn by Mother and Grandma, both of whom had stayed home. Mother came and went, squatted and skipped, walked and ran in a constant race against the sun, scanning the steppe for us and, whenever she caught sight of us, reporting to Grandma, who would then size up the situation and pass judgment.

When I got back, I described like any shepherd in great detail what had happened during the course of the day. I always told what I had seen and observed, sticking to the facts although sometimes allowing myself a little exaggeration. So I claimed that the eagle had attacked us and that we had fought it off. I did so less to get praise for myself than for Arsylang. In the end, we both got praised and I was sent to play. But I did not feel like playing. The praise stuck, mouth-warm, in my ears and urged me on to further action. So I decided to search my *hendshe* for ticks. I combed the lambs' necks with my fingers and crushed whatever ticks I found. Generally, the ticks went for the neck artery. They would pierce the skin and sink their teeth into it, and then suck up blood until they were full, thick as a finger, and bluish-purple. One was not allowed to tear them off because the cold might seep into the wound they left behind. Instead, one was to crush them and leave them in place. In time, the new skin would cast them off anyway.

Ticks filled with blood were easier to crush: they went *pop*. And the louder the pop, the bigger the praise. Sometimes when I hit on a particularly large number of ticks, or on ticks that were only half full and hard to crush, Father came to my aid.

But the best part was washing my hands afterward. Piece by piece the meat which had kept my senses alert all evening was taken from the broth in the kettle and stacked on a platter, forming a pile that steamed so much that the yurt nearly went dark for a moment. That was the signal to wash my hands and get ready. Then I would proudly show off my blood-smeared fingers and say: "I can't grab the can!" And Grandma would offer: "Let me pour the water over your hands." With a casual air, I would hold my hands under the lukewarm juniper water that glittered and gurgled from the water can's spigot. I would wash finger after finger and then the backs of my hands and my wrists and further up. I would listen to the splashing and crashing sounds and strive to create even more sounds—sounds, if possible, like those I had heard when Father washed his hands, and through it all I would feel happy in the anticipation of being a grown-up.

That evening Grandma squatted behind the stove as usual and tended the fire. Half a step away from his regular seat, Father sat close to the oil lamp and bent over the remains of a piece of raw yak skin he was cutting into straps. Just as close to the lamp and just as bent over, Mother was sewing a fox-fur hat. It had blue silk on the outside and brownish-red satin on the inside. What little light remained fell on the yurt's right side where Grandma's bed was already prepared. At its foot a big basket sat upside down and covered over. Instead of dung, it contained several prematurely born lambs. At the edge of the light I was busy removing ticks from a year-old lamb. But my thoughts were not with the lamb or its ticks. They were chasing the big flock that would come together one day, and approaching the question as to who would own it. I wanted clarity:

"Our flock will grow, won't it, Grandma?"

"Of course it will," she responded in a soft, rich voice.

"And how big do you think it might get?"

"Even a single lamb can beget a flock of a thousand, my father used to say."

"Will I be a *baj* when it reaches a thousand?"

Grandma hesitated with her answer. So, she suspected what I was after. Mother and Father stayed silent, too. They concentrated on their work and had said little all evening.

I waited for a while, but then lost my patience. "I shall be a *baj*!" I said.

"*Baj* can also mean simply rich. Anybody who works hard and spares no effort can get rich."

That was Grandma, and Father nodded at her.

"No, Grandma. No, Father. I don't just want to get rich. I want to be a real *baj*. Like Grandfather."

I noticed how Father paused. But again it was Grandma who answered: "Your grandfather was an outstanding man. Happy the person who will be as he was. But these days we no longer speak of *bajs*: we call them Champion Herders."

So that was it. I was not going to be a *baj*, I was going to be a Champion Herder instead. I was disappointed. But I was also relieved to at least know what I would be.

"I shall be a Champion Herder, and you shall be a Champion Dog," I said to Arsylang on our way to the pasture the following morning. Then I added: "Well, what can you do? That's how it goes." All the people in the Altai mountains knew this phrase, which had probably been around forever. Much has disappeared, but some things have endured.

After the first slaughter Father took food to the *sum*. Four frozen blocks of meat from small animals made up the advance payment. Brother and Sister would not be able to eat that much by themselves, so any leftovers would go to the people who had put them up.

The food lay heavy on the horse's back. In addition to the blocks of frozen meat, there was white and yellow butter in wether rumens and in yak bladders, and frozen disks of yak milk the size and shape of our kettle. The horse staggered when he set off.

Father did not return until evening. He brought sweets with him. They came from Brother and Sister, who had both learned well, winning awards at the end of the first quarter. There were two glacier-white lumps of sugar, both larger than my fists, and three candies in blue-striped wrappers. One was thinner and brighter than the other two, and Brother Galkaan later confessed he had sucked it a little. They were the very first candies I ever saw. All the sweets were wrapped in a white cloth, which was also an award and was covered with rows of square dimples. It looked like a piece of wether rumen. Later I learned that it was called a face-and-hand cloth, and later still, I was awarded one myself. Father spread the cloth and broke one of the lumps by tapping it with the back of his dagger. With each further tap the pieces broke into smaller bits. The grown-ups wanted just a taste and in the end were content with the crumbs. They told me to eat all I could. But I didn't eat more than a few little splinters. I could have eaten more of course, I could have finished it all, but I didn't want the sweets to be gone. How much better to look at them and touch them, to sniff and lick them whenever

I felt like it! Each morning before leaving the yurt I unwrapped the cloth and looked at its contents. Often I would content myself with a look and a sniff, but sometimes I would lick them to assure myself of their sweet taste, only to pull myself together quickly and put away the bundle.

The second quarter was said to be over soon, and that meant Brother and Sister would be returning. I counted the days, but the fewer were left, the longer they seemed to become. I was sure that Arsylang already knew. Not surprisingly, he felt my excitement; day after day my stories had dealt with Brother and Sister, and he got excited each time I mentioned their names. We lived in anticipation of seeing them again. In other words: we suffered.

Finally the time had come. Father saddled two horses, took one by its lead, and rode off. It was early in the day, and the sun had only just risen. My eyes were glued to the gelding with his empty saddle. The thought that he would bring Brother and Sister back to me before sunset shook me. I decided that if he returned with them, I would honor the bay—whom we called Scholak Dorug, or the brown one with the stumpy tail—as if he were my own brother. I kept my word. I never humiliated him although later I could not avoid making him pant and sweat. But because I always respected him, he must have sensed how I felt toward him. In turn, he behaved impeccably toward me and served me reliably. When we saw each other for the last time, Scholak Dorug was standing in the midst of a large herd, rested and well fed. The summer sun reflected off his mane onto me. It was the sun of the eighteenth summer of both our lives — for we were of the same age. I was, as people say, at the beginning of my path, but his path had almost reached its end, and so he spent his last summer enjoying his life's holiday: At the beginning of spring, his saddle had been removed for good. I knew we would never see each other again, and I was grateful to the people who had created the custom of paying one's last respects to old, worn-out animals. I sensed that the gelding, too, knew what lay ahead, as his gaze seemed to radiate both pain and gratitude.

The day Brother and Sister were expected to return was one of the longest of my life. It was also one of the hardest, as well as one of the most beautiful. Arsylang and I were told to stay with our flock until Father returned with Scholak Dorug, who would carry Brother and Sister on his back over Doora Hara, the mountain ridge that stretched from right to left at a distance of two or three gun shots below our camp, and that had got its name from looking black.

Mother was walking the large flock along the ridge that formed a half circle high above us on the other side of the camp, above the steep rock face of Gysyl Dshagyr. I could tell that she, too, was looking out for

them, for she and a small tip of her flock appeared repeatedly even though it must have been very windy
up there on the ridge.

Grandma also kept an eye out for them. Again and
again she stepped out of the yurt to stand and look.
We could see her, but I knew that with her aged eyes
she could not see us. So I shouted: "Grand-ma-a, we
are he-re!" and Arsylang barked along. But she just
stood there, stooped and motionless. She obviously
did not hear us. In the morning we had agreed that
whenever she would see or hear us, she would wave
the white yak tail normally used for dusting. But, apparently, Grandma's ears had aged as well.

We kept our eyes trained on Father and followed
him as he became smaller and smaller. Occasionally he
disappeared from view but then showed up again, even
smaller than before and as threadbare as a breeze in a
mirage. But I only had to glance at Arsylang to assure
myself that the figure I saw was indeed still Father. In
his eyes everything was as clear as if it were written.
Behind the fourth of the seven Kazakh homes Father
disappeared again and this time did not re-emerge.
After that, we went off on the wrong track. Each time
we discovered and followed a moving body here, or
another one there, they turned out to be wrong. Only
much later, when the mountains' shadows had reap-
peared and were growing more quickly, did we find
him again, right where we had lost him.

At first it was Arsylang who jumped and whimpered with joy and pain. Then I discovered the grayish-dark speck standing out against the light-brown steppe. It was growing and coming closer. There was no doubt: it was our people! Then I could distinguish the two horses which until then had formed but one dark figure, as well as the riders who had dismounted and were now walking ahead of their horses. They crossed the frozen river and mounted their horses again, and then all of a sudden the two dark figures began to grow.

Arsylang and I made such a racket, jumping up and down and running around in circles, that Mother must have seen us. Together with the little tip of her flock she disappeared from sight and was obviously now heading toward the *ail*. I knew it would take her some time to make her way across the ridge's more gradual northern slope to the saddle and then down from there. Our own flock had already set out for home. All day long we had forced the animals to stay on the windy mountain ridge. The young lambs had begun to bleat and look for protection among last year's lambs, and even the latter, who had turned their heads toward the *ail* and pulled in their legs, were no longer searching for blades of grass. They were cold. While Arsylang and I had been occupied with the events in the steppe beyond the rivers, they had abandoned us and taken off. But from up where we were, we could see them as if in the palm of my hand. They had reached the slope below Eser-Haja, which was sheltered from the wind, and had come to a halt.

By now the riders had left the Ak-Hem valley and were climbing the foothills of the Black Mountains. We didn't know how to stay calm or how to make them progress faster. While I knew that the horses could only go at a walk and had to struggle hard to make ground—surely they were walking too slowly!—I jumped up and down and urged Arsylang to continue to love and honor our father *Gök-Deeri* and our mother *Hara Dsher*, not least for having brought our dear ones back to us safe and sound. Arsylang whimpered and barked and jumped with me. He was trembling all over, and joy lit up his eyes like a bright flame. He would have loved above all to tear off and race toward them. But I knew he would not leave me. Under no circumstances would he ever leave me behind on the lonely mountain ridge.

By then we could see that the horses were being driven hard. They were struggling up the path across the rock face, one behind the other, their necks stretched forward, maintaining their distance from each other. Their dark coats shone with hoarfrost, and both horses were steaming and snorting clouds of breath that quickly rose toward the sky and dissolved in a gray veil. Father rode in front, and he seemed as powerful as always but also decidedly elegant, even beautiful. I vaguely detected a smile on his face, and I also thought I saw smiles on the faces of Brother and Sister. But Torlaa's face looked strangely bright and even somewhat narrow as she sat in the saddle in front of Brother. And Galkaan's face, which peered out two or three times from behind his sister's back, radiated the kind of brightness people in the mountains in those days called "paper-white." Strangers called him Whitey anyway, whereas Sister had been nicknamed Red for her ruddy cheeks, and I Blackey, for reasons I never understood.

With his skin tone, Brother Galkaan took after Father, who with his light skin, hook nose, brown hair, and his round, light-brown eyes was a rarity among Tuvans. Father showed, as I would later learn, Caucasian traces.

When they got close enough for me to recognize their features and indeed their smiles, I suddenly felt timid. I had no idea where the feeling came from or what it meant, but I felt it so clearly that I would have given anything to run away. But how and where? I stayed where I was. No longer jumping or rejoicing, I stood as if paralyzed, and all I could do was whisper to Arsylang: "Please be quiet . . . please be quiet!"

They arrived with much hullabaloo. Just as they were taking their very last step, Arsylang seemed to lose his patience, which he had probably adopted only for my sake anyway. He charged at them and with his front paws climbed up on Brother and Sister, at which Torlaa let out a shrill scream while Arsylang howled and whimpered. With his body stretched and his ears flattened, he hung on to them and sniffed and licked them all over. Torlaa wouldn't stop screaming. Father shouted to her: "Don't worry. He isn't going to hurt you!" But to no avail: she kept on screaming. I could also hear Brother Galkaan's voice, but at least his was less a scream than an expression of pleasure and likely was meant to greet Arsylang. Yet even Galkaan seemed to find it unbearable to be licked by the dog's tongue. He pulled away and raised his right arm, which had been around Sister's waist, while his left arm clutched her ever more tightly. I was grateful to Arsylang for the turmoil he had caused because it shielded me from everybody's attention which otherwise might well have been directed at me and which I could not have borne. By then Father had dismounted and walked up to me. He sniffed my forehead where the hair peered out, clasped my ice-cold cheeks with his lukewarm hands, and said: "Oh, my dear stupid little one, you've spent all day up here, haven't you?" I wanted to say— wanted to lie—that we had only just arrived, but my tongue failed me. Perhaps the cold had crept into my tongue, but whatever the case may be, all of a sudden I was lifted off the ground, carried over to Brother and Sister, and held first in front of Sister and then in front of Brother so they could sniff me. And so they did, although with both it was just a brief sniffing and did not really compare with the sniffing that grown-ups gave you. But that was fine with me, as I was dying with embarrassment and made myself rigid and even closed my eyes when I saw their faces so close to me. I sniffed them back regardless: They gave off something foreign, something gloriously pleasant. It was the scent that came off the *dargas* and the elegant people from the country's interior.

Then, fortunately, I was carried to Father's horse and put in its saddle. Soon after, Father swung himself up as well. At last I felt relief and could now secretly watch the two. They had become pale and slim and very, very talkative: They talked almost as if they were competing, calling the rocks, slopes, hollows, saddles, and paths each by their name, and finding everything in its place. And when we rode past our small flock, which by then had left its wind-sheltered hideout and set out on its journey home, they also called out the names—which were mostly nicknames—of the yearlings together with those of their mothers. Arsylang, too, behaved strangely. He raced wildly in all directions, but always returned.

Sometimes he even came up to the horse, jumped up its side, and reached the knees of Brother or Sister with his front paws or even his mouth. And each time he did, we could hear Sister Torlaa's anxious screams.

Once we had reached the yurt and dismounted, he behaved even more strangely. Brother Galkaan had hardly set foot on the ground when Arsylang dropped down and rolled about next to him. He followed Brother around, his tail wagging and his eyes burning. Then he would jump up again, place his front paws on Brother's shoulders, sniff and lick him, and howl and whimper. Brother tried to fend off the paws that seemed to want to grip his neck like two hands. But he also was giggling, and for that I was grateful— not only for Arsylang's sake, but also for my own. After all, my four-legged companion, my brother-instead-of-a-brother, was acting out my own feelings toward my real brother. I, too, would have so loved to grab Brother, drop to the ground with him, and roll about! But the bashfulness that all of a sudden had risen like a whirlwind and was now almost choking me had not yet left, and so I had to wait.

Toward Sister I felt some hurt. Although I was glad that she had come back to us safe and sound, back to her yurt, her flock, and her mountains, I felt some hurt which was neither excruciating nor bitter, but nevertheless sharp like a stab: Why could she not bear Arsylang's outburst of joy, his joyful greeting which expressed my own joy as well as the joy of the flock and the mountains? Arsylang was not only the most capable of us all, but also the most dignified to give voice to all our amassed, pent up joy and to offer the pent up greeting. I felt hurt by Sister and in my mind called her an idiot even though at the same time I was sensing my love for her more strongly than ever. It was her fault that, for the time being at least, the whole affair ended when Father called out and threatened the dog, and then bent over and grabbed a stone. But he no longer needed to throw the stone because the dog had already fled, and so the stone flew without heart and only vaguely in the same direction. Arsylang did not seem to have taken the threat or the stone too seriously in any case, because when Torlaa stepped out of the yurt soon afterward, the dog slinked back with all his doggish loveliness on display. But she just ran back into the yurt with more screams of fear. Somebody had to chase the dog away and keep him at a distance, as if we had strangers visiting who needed to relieve themselves. But this was true only for the first day.

Grandma could not help but cry when she saw Brother and Sister, and she chided herself for it. It was the first time I saw her cry. "Oh, my rich Altai!" she said, "the yurt is full again!" Then she sniffed both their heads, paused, and stroked them several times with a trembling hand before letting them go.

Later the two of them sat on either side of Grandma and talked about school and everything they had seen and heard, again as if competing with each other.

The jealousy I had suffered in the past when Brother and Sister moved too close to Grandma seemed cured—I no longer felt it. On the contrary, I was grateful to all three of them for being kind to each other.

Mother lost her voice when she first saw Brother and Sister. She simply stared at them with glistening eyes. When she regained her voice, her words were not aimed at her children but at the sky, the mountains, and the rivers. Brother and Sister stood with their heads bowed while Mother sniffed them. They did not say a word. To me they seemed to avoid being close to Mother in the beginning. But after a little while, they would not leave her side.

I had counted on more sweets and possibly also a new cloth, even though the old one still lay brand-new in our chest of drawers, wrapped around the remaining sugar. Now I realized that I had indeed relied on this new cloth and had thought ahead about giving up the old one for the parents to dry their faces and hands. But for the time being my expectations remained unfulfilled. This was not because Brother and Sister had done less well at school; no, both had finished the quarter with very good results and had again been given an award, although now it was called a present. The top students were going to be given their presents by the Old White Man under the *jolka* in the evening. But Father had not wanted to wait till evening and then have to ride home during the night; it was because of us waiting in the *ail* that he had not stayed. The mere idea that they might not have made it home by sunset made me feel sick and took the luster off the Old White Man's presents. Nevertheless, I cautiously asked if this meant that the presents were now lost. No, I was told, the teachers would receive and keep them and later pass them on to those for whom they were intended. That was good.

I knew of course who the Old White Man was. He came the night before the New Year and lifted the children to check if they had eaten well. He threw away those who had not eaten enough and rewarded those who had with even more delicious dishes. So far, nobody in our clan had been thrown away, but people said it had happened elsewhere. But I did not know what the *jolka* was. Father could not tell me and not even Grandma knew. Brother and Sister talked about a decorated room, but did not know what exactly it was all about. Much later I learned that *jolka* was derived from a Russian word and meant Christmas tree. At the time, our New Year celebrations had not yet been declared illegal, but preparations for that step were well under way, and new customs were gaining ground. Even in our corner of the country, people had begun to celebrate New Year's Eve the way people did in Russia, and the Russian Father Frost had become the Mongolian Old White Man.

I was not the Old White Man, but I did serve Brother and Sister the leftover sweets they had been awarded before. They were more astonished than pleased. Sister Torlaa wanted to know why I had not been allowed to eat them. "It was his own choice," Mother explained, "he was very frugal." Was she defending herself or making excuses for me? "You'll become a Stalin," said Sister Torlaa, only to be scolded. The chiding came from Father and included a rebuke for Mother, who had coined the phrase everybody now used when they found fault with me. On the other hand, Brother Galkaan had nothing but praise: "That's amazing! I couldn't have done it." It was costly praise: I gave him the biggest piece, and he ate it with relish. Days later, though, I got the replacement when Father returned with the Old White Man's presents after taking Brother and Sister back to school.

They had kept nothing for themselves and sent me everything that was in the two paper bags. There were candies and biscuits of a kind nobody had ever seen. The biscuits tasted slightly of roasted barley flour and were soft and very sweet. Grandma praised them, but I said I couldn't eat them. So Grandma ate the soft, sweet biscuits and loudly blessed Brother and Sister, who had learned well and earned their presents.

Brother and Sister stayed with us for nine days. I spent my days with Brother and my nights with Sister. It was the first time I sensed in him a second father and in her a second mother. They pampered me. Once again I was the baby. But my time with them was far too short. It was like a dream I had to wake up from in order to become aware that I had been deeply happy. I had to wake up and watch Brother and Sister be torn from me again. Arsylang watched along with me, and I realized only then that I must have somehow neglected him over the days of their visit. I felt guilty. Dark sadness filled his eyes as he carefully watched Father saddle the horses and tie the bulging bags to the saddles. When Father lifted Brother and Sister up onto their horse and Mother sprinkled milk on their stirrups, Arsylang plunked himself on his behind, turned his mouth toward the sky, and let out a low, drawn-out howl.

"Oh, you stupid mutt!" Mother said and looked around anxiously. Father bent down, grabbed a stone, and in one motion hurled it. Having put himself into a trance with his own howling, Arsylang noticed the stone coming his way only at the very last moment, and had just enough time to be startled. As the stone hit him in the side with a dull thud, he cried out and dragged himself away. Staggering clumsily, he let out an unbroken sound like the sobbing of a deeply aggrieved child.

Grandma had just touched Torlaa's left knee with her palm and was about to do the same with Galkaan's; she had already sniffed them when they were still on the ground. Now she shook her head and said: "Oh Schynyk, why did you do that? To make the poor creature scream and howl instead of offering him some milk—that's silly!" Then she touched Brother's knee, rested her hand on it for a moment, and stepped back. Arsylang was still sobbing as he slinked away. He trotted over to the big rock where we slaughtered the cattle and horses, crouched down in front of it with his tail between his legs, and howled at the sky. His howling quickly became unbearable, and everybody, big or small, was petrified and did not know what to do. Finally Grandma shook off her paralysis and told me to fetch the milk pail from the yurt. Behind me, I heard her call after Arsylang. When I returned with the pail, everybody but Father was shouting in unison: "Arsylang, Arsylang, Arsylang, Arsylang, mäh!" Mäh meant: "Come here, have some!" which is how Tuvan dogs have always been, and still are, lured close. But Arsylang would not listen and kept on howling, and so I was told to take him the bowl with some milk. Arsylang squinted at me suspiciously as I got closer, even as he continued howling. I reached him, put the milk in front of him, and squatted down. Arsylang did not move and howled on.

"What's the matter?" I heard Mother call out impatiently.

"He's already got the milk!" I shouted back.

Father, who through all this had been fidgeting with the seams of Brother's and Sister's *tons*, went over to his horse. Then they set off. Finally, Mother was able to sprinkle the milk that she had kept ready in her ladle all this time after the parting riders. I was still squatting and had turned only halfway to see what was going on behind me. One moment I followed those who were leaving and the next, those who were staying behind. Arsylang continued to howl, but his howling did not grow louder. Suddenly I noticed a small bright sphere of tear hanging off the lower rim of one of his small dark eyes. I had never before seen Arsylang or any other dog cry—I did not even know that my Arsylang, or any dog, could cry like me, like any human being, or like a mare or a yak. The sphere of tear dropped and disappeared in the frozen snow. I needed to comfort him, so I moved closer and stuck my freezing hands into his shaggy neck hair. Suddenly I felt how violently he was shivering, and it made me shiver, too. The need to sob and to shudder in pro-test at all that was happening in this world against my will overcame me. It was so overwhelming that all my good intentions could no longer hold back the tears that had already filled my eyes and were blurring my vision. And so I cried, and in crying, I knew that I, too, would have to go away one day. I wanted to stay among my mountains, to guard my flock and become a herder as Father was and as everybody had been who lived before him in our world. I wanted to stay with Arsylang: staying with him was the least I could do after all he had done for me. And I wanted to have a yurt of my own in which I could live with Grandma so

I would never have to leave her. And finally, I had to keep an eye on my parents since I could see how much they depended on me doing my share of the work and simply being there: I was their youngest, their most beloved child, and in the end I would have to take care not only of Grandma but also of them.

The day was hard. The cold that had lingered from the previous night continued to sting. Pale and distant and small, the sun was too weak to break it. The world seemed empty as it glittered with hoarfrost, and I felt abandoned. As a companion, Arsylang seemed inadequate to me, a mere substitute, and I sensed that I was not enough for him either.

The big flock appeared earlier than I had expected at the upper end of the path which—bright and wide like a glacier's arm and surrounded by a half circle of rocks that formed a ridge above the *ail* as sharp as a knife's edge—seemed to plummet from the saddle toward the *hürde*. But this only depressed me further. Had everything, each and every thing, fallen into disarray on this cold, empty earth that glittered with hoarfrost?

I picked out Mother trailing along behind the herd as it streamed down the steep slope like a wide river. She seemed small and round and moved awkwardly like a child dressed in too many clothes. Even though it pained me, I could not take my eyes off her for a long time. And all the time I watched her, the lack of understanding I carried within me continued to grow and to spread.

Father did not come back until night had fallen. Arsylang announced his return well in advance; he barked without getting up and without haste or enthusiasm. Even though it must have been quite late when Father finally arrived, I was still awake. Was it only his absence that had kept me restless? Hardly, for I did not cheer up afterward either, not even when Father unpacked the gift he had brought: the sweets and the hand-and-face cloth from the Old White Man. For a while I held the rough, strange-smelling, shining white cloth with its pile of sweets in my hands the way one holds the blue or white ceremonial scarves. But then I put it aside without having tasted anything. I watched Father, who was bent over the platter and eating meat. And I listened to what he told us, but I was unable to keep my thoughts together. They soon left the yurt and went out into the steppe and into the mountain valleys, where rustling cold, glittering hoarfrost, and loneliness awaited me.

The next morning Grandma said: "Dusky's time is up!" Dusky was the one remaining wether that had come to us with Grandma's flock. Did this mean that now this animal, too, would be taken from the flock and from the earth?

But why? The shelf outside with the winter provisions was full of meat. The restlessness I had felt the previous day but that seemed to have vanished during the night awoke in me again. I was on my guard and watched closely what was happening around me.

My fear was justified: Father was about to slaughter Dusky and was in a hurry because he also had to look after the flock. I was told to help him, which meant I had to hold the victim's hind legs. Horrified, I watched Father fight with the big, strong animal until he finally threw it over and slammed his right leg across its belly. I reached for the kicking hind legs where they were thinnest and grabbed and pulled them toward me as I fell backward and shoved my legs against the wether's rear end. I didn't mean to, but I couldn't avoid watching Father's right hand grope for the sheath at his belt. I saw the naked steel flash, saw its tip appear to graze Dusky's belly just below the breastbone, leaving behind a slit beyond which, before its edges turned dark, white rumen fat became visible. And then I saw the hand drop the knife and thrust, with fingers straight and pressed together, into the slit as a hawk charges at a sparrow. I saw and felt how the animal twitched and started to spasm, and how immensely its strength grew as I fought to hold on. I knew that under no circumstances could I let go of the ankles I was holding away from the body, so I clenched my teeth and tightened my tendons. Dusky's

struggle lasted for some time, maybe one whole min-
ute. When at long last the animal faded and I felt its
strength grow weaker breath by breath and then die
away altogether, I watched the lifeless legs slide from
my hands. They stood motionless in the air above the
belly, like stumps of dead branches.

Then I knew that I no longer had a Dusky, that
there was no longer any Dusky, not in the flock and
not on the earth. Only a pile of meat remained, and
that would not be there much longer either.

Grandma told me to drive the flock toward the
mountain saddle around noon, and then to come home
for some of the meat that by then would be cooked.
But I did not go home, although I was hungry and had
only the handful of rock-hard pieces of curd cheese
that I carried in my breast pocket next to the glow
stone. I did not want that meat. With horror and revulsion I thought back to the slaughter. I remembered
details of Dusky's end that I had not properly regis-
tered at the time, such as how urine had poured out
after the hand disappeared inside the slit and pressed
deeper and deeper, apparently searching for whatever
it was that had to be severed.

The cold endured. The lambs born late in the fall
could no longer walk or look for grass. Again and again
they paused and just stood there trembling, each
pressed against the others and withdrawn into itself.
I shooed them apart and drove them on so that they

would not freeze to death. I was terribly cold myself, but in contrast to the lambs I understood that I had to keep moving in order not to die from the cold. I also had the glow stone, which was now of real use: for me it was a small sun.

Arsylang walked behind me and seemed to cower as if lying in wait. From time to time our eyes met, and I noticed that he was waiting for a sign from me. But I could not find the strength to break the barrier that had come between us.

When I got home in the evening, I found the kettle full of meat. It struck me as insane that so much meat had been cooked, particularly since Dusky had had to die for it. Grandma, who had already lain down, wanted to know if the flock had not left me enough time all day for a quick run home. It had not, I agreed. But when I saw the steaming meat piled high on the platter with all its pieces clearly showing, I could no longer hold back. The smell was too strong, too enticing. Gone was the revulsion I had felt all day and even just then; my hunger was stronger. I greedily tore into the pile and gorged on the meat. It was strange, though, that the fuller my stomach grew, the duller my senses became, and in the end I was no longer aware that the delicious meat had come from Dusky, whose frisky, proud looks had delighted my eyes for so long, and whose glorious image I had lent a helping hand to extinguish.

The next morning I noticed that Grandma was bedridden. She continued to tell her little stories about everyday life in years gone by, and the gentle smile in her old, wrinkled face accompanied the telling.

Dusky, she recounted, had been an orphan lamb whose mother was eaten by a wolf just after his birth. Grandma had noticed that the ewe was missing and went looking for her. When she finally found her, the ewe's body lay in the snow while the trembling lamb stood at her side. It had almost frozen to death and was hungry because it hadn't had its first milk. Grandma noticed the swollen, unscathed udder, touched it, and found it lukewarm; the wolf had probably taken off when she arrived. So Grandma crouched down and held the lamb to the udder. The poor thing had been looking for the mother's udder, and now it quickly found the tit and began to suck. After it had drunk from the other tit as well, its desperate thirst seemed quenched. Grandma tucked the orphaned lamb in the breast pocket of her coat and started home. First she could sense its cold and later its warmth, and when she got home and pulled the lamb from her coat, she found it sleeping peacefully. She swaddled it like a baby and took it to her own bed for the night. The next morning the lamb was given a new mother. It stayed alive and thrived. Drinking the first milk from its mother's udder had been good for it because that milk was thick and shimmered golden. Anybody unable to drink his fill of

the first milk fails to thrive, and this is true for all living beings. There is a reason the first milk is called fire
milk. "Eat of the meat and drink of the broth," Grandma
concluded. "The orphan lamb became a wether and
the lonely woman a mother with a yurt full of children—how could it have turned out better?"

The following night I woke up suddenly. A fire was burning in the stove, and the *dshula* was lit in the *dör* even
though the oil lamp was burning as well. Grandma sat
propped against a tall pillow made of rolled-up clothes.
Father and Mother sat at either side of her. Grandma
spoke and Father and Mother listened quietly while
looking at each other. Grandma was talking about two
dung baskets that were to be put bottom-up, about
her clothes, and about a body that would feel neither
pain nor cold.

"You know that, Schynyk, don't you?" she said and
paused, but Father did not respond. So she continued: "Burn all the clothes; that's the cleanest way." Although I heard the words and saw Grandma say them,
I could not grasp what they meant. The bit about the
dung baskets and the body struck me as even more
mysterious since I had not heard what had been said
when I was still asleep.

Then she gave her blessings. They were for Father
and Mother and their children, and for all the people

in the *ail* and in the *aimag*. Afterward she began to sing the praises of the Altai and its mountains, steppes, valleys, rivers, lakes, and forests, and of the sky above. Having heard them from the grown-ups and used them myself when I had the opportunity, I had long known these hymns by heart, so I noticed that Grandma confused a few lines. They were meant to praise the sky but suddenly addressed the earth.

It much astonished me because such a mistake was not unheard of with other people, but it certainly was with Grandma. Yet I listened with delight and even piety and conviction to everything that was said in the quiet of the night in the dim, quivering light of the quiet dung fire, oil lamp, and *dshula*. Then her voice broke off, and I thought Grandma wanted to sigh because she breathed out loudly, and then sucked in her breath equally loudly and slowly. Then there was quiet. This was a different quiet from the one that had been there before in small fragments and had filled the breaks between Grandma's lines. Cold and hot waves of this quiet that now resembled a void washed over me—I could feel the heat and the cold as clearly as if I had sat between the burning stove and the open door. But this quiet did not last long. Father broke it: *"Höörküj awam dshoj bardy oj!"*—Poor sister has left!

He had whispered loudly, which may be why it sounded frightening, as if he had hissed. Mother jumped: *"Uj dshüü didri sen?!"*—Oh, what are you saying?

These two exclamations of shock are locked in my memory like incantations, and, along with rhymes, proverbs, songs, and other well-shaped sayings, have accompanied me through life without being dulled by the passage of time, without losing their rough edges and thus becoming crippled or a deformed and impassive mass.

I sat up. I wanted to see better and to find out for sure whether Grandma had really left, as Father had just claimed, or was still there, as it seemed to me. I saw that she still sat there and was leaning back with her eyes closed as if in thought. At that moment Father noticed me. He gestured to Mother, who came over, pulled me back by my shoulders, tucked me into the fur *ton* I had lain in before, and whispered firmly: "Stay put and go back to sleep!" She took my rolled-up *ton*, which had served her as a pillow, and placed it in front of my head to block my view.

Bewildered and cowed, I could not find the courage to push aside the *ton*. Instead I lay still and listened. There was nothing for me to do but pick up the sounds of what was happening on the other side and translate them into what my other senses might take in. And so I figured that Grandma was being undressed and her clothes bundled up, that Mother was sewing something. . . . Then I was overcome by sleep. . . .

I woke up late. Father and Mother had not called and shaken me as usual, but had let me sleep and wake up on my own. The first things I noticed were the roof ring and the top ends of the ribs holding it in place. Blazing sunlight was streaming into the yurt. Then I saw the shining blue of the sky beyond the roof hole. Both the sunlight and the sky struck me as strange, as if I had searched for them and longed to see them again, and as if something had occurred to me that I now had to tell them about. My eyes wandered to where Grandma used to sit and slurp her tea from her wooden bowl when I heard the wake-up call and felt the wake-up shake, and when I fought equally against the call, the shake, and my sleep, and then finally opened my eyes.

But this time Grandma was not there. Her bedside had been cleared. The three sheep skins piled on top of each other which she used to sit on were no longer there.

Her cane was nowhere to be seen, either. Instead of Grandma and instead of her things I saw Dügürshep. He was the older of Nansyka's two sons and the father of the other Torlaa, the one who was called Little Torlaa then and Pale Torlaa later. Ours was called Red. Nansyka's *ail* always spent the winter in Hany Dsharyk, the mountain valley next to ours. Sometimes we noticed smoke or heard the dogs bark over there, but so far none of us had had the heart to go there. Now this Dügürshep was sitting and eating in our *dör*. Father sat next to him and ate with him. Mother was busy in the kitchen area and talked while she worked. She was talking about someone who had explained long ago that she would announce when her time had come, and who now had announced that her time had come. And it had been true.

I got up, slipped into my boots and *ton*, put on my belt, and stepped outside. I did not say a word and neither did the others. The *hürde* was empty. The tip of a flock was just disappearing behind the mountain finger below Eser-Haja. It must have been the *hendshe*. Arsylang was nowhere to be seen. For the first time ever I went all the way to the rocks behind which the adults went to relieve themselves. I went there even though I knew I was allowed to pee anywhere I wanted—I could have peed walking or even skipping had I been in the mood. But my mind was not on playing now, nor on being the youngest, the only child in the *ail*. The horses were saddled and shone with the hoarfrost that covered their bodies. Who might ride off with Scholak Dorug?

All our horses were tame, but this one was the tamest. Even when we moved and Scholak Dorug was loaded, we could let go of his reins and drive him before us with the oxen. Now he stood there with my saddle on his back, with a piece of felt serving as a blanket beneath it that reached all the way down to his belly. Was he about to be loaded? Outside, there were two dung baskets sitting where none had sat before. The previous night, one had contained *desgen* roots, while the other one, empty and upside down, had been covered with Dusky's skin, which had been put outside, frozen stiff, to dry in the cold. But now both baskets stood empty next to the stone altar for smoke offerings, diligently lined up as if after a day's work. I also saw signs of a fourth horse. They were tracks left by small hooves, the front ones apparently having been shoed recently.

Without having to be reminded, I washed my hands and even my face. Usually I avoided washing my face in the morning by claiming that I would have to scrub it with snow many times during the day to avoid frostbite when I was out with the flock. In reality, however, I scrubbed my face very rarely—only when my cheeks or my chin, or the tip of my nose, were actually close to being frostbitten. After such a quick snow wash, at first I would briefly feel colder than before, but as soon as the skin dried, I would feel warmth or sometimes even a little rush of heat, as if a tiny animal were stirring in the pores of my skin.

There was freshly cooked meat even though the meat from the day before could not possibly have been finished. There were even grains of rice floating in the broth, which on any other day would have made me delirious. I was soon full and left right afterward

for my flock. Nobody made me do so, but then nobody tried to stop me, either. Nobody said anything
to me that mattered in any way. And nobody told me
what had happened to Grandma and where she had
gone. Maybe it was better this way; after all, nothing would have felt more terrible than a conversation
about Grandma. But at the same time I wanted badly
to know what had happened to her and where she
was now.

I caught up with the flock in Gysyl Göschge after it had already turned around. Arsylang was running along its far side. When he saw me, he ran toward
me. He reached me at full speed, drew a narrow circle
around me, threw himself on the ground in front of me,
and whimpered quietly. Did he know? What a question—of course he knew!

Maybe he had even been there with her?

"Arsylang! Where's Grandma?"

The dog jumped up, turned his head toward the
west, scanned it sharply, pricked up his ears—and remained in this position. I sensed that if I were to ask
him again where Grandma was, or better still, if I were
to call for her so that the rocks around us would echo
my voice, *En-eeej! En-eej!* . . . , my four-legged companion would immediately squat on his behind, point his
jaws at the sky, and fall into a drawn-out, terrifying
howling. That was something I did not want to happen under any circumstances. I was afraid of Arsylang,

afraid of myself, and afraid of whatever it was that had happened around us and that I would eventually hear about. I also sensed that if I were to run in the direction in which he was staring and were to call over and over, Tuh! Tuh! Tuh! . . . , he would come along, run a little ahead of me, and take me there. That was what I most feared.

I would have dearly loved to know what had happened to Grandma, but I was afraid to hear the truth, afraid to look eye to eye with a truth that was bound to be heavy, hard, and bitter. I suspected what might have happened to Grandma in spite of all that she had talked me into believing only yesterday, or the day before yesterday, or the day before that, day after day. Having a suspicion was agonizing, but I preferred living with uncertainty as it still meant a ray of hope.

When I returned with my flock to the *hürde* and the yurt in the evening, I learned who had taken care of the large flock: Galdarak, Dügürshep's younger brother. He was drinking tea and eating meat, and telling what he had seen in the course of the day, where the wind had blown from, and how the flock had behaved. Then he rode off.

I was left alone with Father and Mother. For the first time ever our family was that small. I pretended to be busy, crushing a lot of ticks, and spent the evening with all my senses alert. But not a word was said about Grandma, who had lain on her bed and worked on the continuation of her stories just the evening before. Now we lived as if we had never had her, never known her.

While I bent over the lambs, combing their necks with my fingers for ticks and crushing a few more, I could still hear her soft, sonorous voice, and I could see the kindly, spider-web smile in her wrinkled face.

As time passed, the secret got more and more hazy. An occasional visitor would ask me teasingly where my grandma with the shaved head had gone. Or sometimes they would be even more direct and ask if I longed for my grandma, who had gone into the salt.

Oh yes, going into the salt! I already knew about that. Once we expected a baby to come to us. We had longed for it so badly but never got to see it. People eventually said that it had lost its way and gone into the salt instead of to us.

Salt was a rarity in those days. People went into the salt with their camels. It took them a long time to return, and when they finally did, they brought back a lot of salt. People also shared whatever salt they had. I often had to run to the neighbors to ask for a bowl of salt, and sometimes I came back with only half a bowl.

I never replied to questions about Grandma. Mother did it for me, or Father. They said that Grandma would return once I was a grown-up. Everybody agreed, even people who had teased me at first.

It was strange, but the doubt that had reared up inside me and torn at their words would then die down, and I would be calmed again for the time being.

I had to stay calm and wait, although naturally my brain was not yet capable of this clear and complete thought in those days. Nevertheless, I must have had this insight in some shape or form, for I remained tame and calm, not only in light of what had already happened, but also in light of what was still to come. I remained resigned to fate—in complete contrast to my nature. But it was good that Arsylang and I were close again. We took care of the flock with each other and for each other. Diligently, we did our duty: Watching over our little flock gave meaning to our life.

It was also good to know that Brother and Sister would return. Not so good was the fact that they would have to leave again, and that they would always have to leave again. And that was not the end of it. I could feel myself growing more and more upset because before long it would be my turn to leave behind the flock, Arsylang, our home, Father and Mother, the Black Mountains—everything that had been part of me. With that thought came misgivings that led to further thoughts and left me afraid: Would Grandma find me if I were no longer at home? What would come of our flock, which meanwhile had become my flock? What of the yurt we would have to get somehow and in which I had planned to live with Grandma? Would I one day become a teacher or even a *darga* and live off a salary rather than livestock? In that case, would I live in a shack made from larch logs and smeared with clay, just like the elegant people in the *sum* center? Which meant, didn't it, that I would never have a yurt of my own, would never put it up and take it down and move with it through the four seasons and across the four rivers, from the mountains into the steppe, over to the other mountains, to the lake, and back? And did this mean that I would have to leave behind, and would never be able to return to, all that I had had and held so far, and all that had been mine?

These and similar thoughts populated my head. They came to me like ragged shadows, settled down in the midst of my life, stayed, and at some point left again without me noticing. I lived my life as it was given to me. What existed in the past had certainly been beautiful, and I loved to remember it. But I had no desire to bring back what was gone. Intuitively I must have known that I had to cling to what still was mine: my flock and my dog.

The Year of the Yellow Cow was coming to its end. Like all years before and quite a few after, it consisted of four parts that were called seasons and followed one another. They appeared to crash into each other like the yurt's folding lattice walls, probably because the events making up the nomadic life differed so harshly from one season to the next.

It was still during the Yellow Cow that we moved to Ulug Gyschtag, our big winter camp. It lay a ridge and two passes farther into the mountains, which meant getting even farther away from people, but closer to whatever was left of the pastures. And the latter was important not least because of the pregnant animals that were trudging wearily beneath the burden of their swelling fruit, and becoming noticeably skinnier.

ARSYLANG

The Cow was followed by the Tiger. Secretly we were afraid of the Tiger, but we didn't forget to look for something to comfort us: This Tiger was white. It was as if the White Tiger came creeping on soft paws, for it was silent before and after. The New Year was not as it used to be. Rumor had it that bleeding dysentery was on its way. Nobody from outside came to visit, and there seemed to be no end to the meat and the deep-fried bread the Yellow Cow had prepared and left for the White Tiger. And even though the New Year and with it the first month of spring had arrived, it was bitterly cold. Snow fell on the ninth and again on the seventeenth.

The second snowfall had been forecast by Father and therefore expected by everybody.

"How much worse will it be on the twenty-second?" everybody wondered. People were on their guard and went about their days with quiet mindfulness. It snowed during the night of the twenty-first. The heavy snowfall did not stop until the following noon and was followed by a storm. The snow already on the ground started to move again, and sky and earth collapsed into each other. The *dshut* had arrived. We took the big flock to where the small one normally grazed. The *hendshe* stayed where it had spent the night and later in the day was fed the way young lambs are fed in their first year: we hung bundles of hay on a line drawn tight above their heads. But when we went to do the same the next day, we had to let the animals off because we did not have enough hay. Mountain and steppe lay in glaring black and white as if shattered in a sea of shards. It tired the eye. And a howling and hissing wind sawed and cut, stung and tugged at everything in its path. The *hendshe* burst into noise when it stepped into this wind.

Driven by the wind, the lambs ran for a while, then tired and tried to hide their heads under one another's bellies for protection from the pinching and stinging cold. They were barely able to graze.

I was cold myself and shivering. The glow stone couldn't keep my hands and face warm. My fingertips burned, along with the backs of my hands, my nose, and my cheeks and chin. And I was freezing in other places as well, such as my calves and my neck.

Even Arsylang kept his tail between his legs and tilted his head when we crossed through the wind that lashed us like flames.

"What on earth shall we do?" I asked Arsylang, pointing at the shivering mass. Arsylang didn't know. So it was left to me to decide. And I decided and said: "Let's go home, Arsylang."

So we drove the flock home. This meant going against the wind, which was hard, but with me shouting and Arsylang barking and both of us running hither and thither, we made progress as best as we could.

Mother was working in the *hürde*, shoveling snow, and digging up and spreading last year's grainy, dry dung in place of the frozen, new dung she had already scraped together in a pile. She looked at me and said: "I had hoped the running would warm them up and make them eat." She sounded unsure of herself, almost apologetic, but then she said in a hard voice as if to admonish or even threaten me: "Grab an armload of hay, but make sure that not a blade is lost in the wind."

The *hendshe* jostled beneath the rock that formed the northern side of the stone wall and jutted out quite a bit above the *hürde*. Under there, the lambs were sheltered from the wind, and all that could be heard now—and more clearly than before—was the rushing and occasional hissing and pelting of the wind. Trembling and murmuring, the *hendshe* tore into the hay, and each of the animals began to eat with a haste I had never seen or thought possible. Mother was watching, too. She told me to fetch *düüleesh* and fresh horse droppings. I took my small basket, slung it over my shoulder, and left with Arsylang. After a while Mother caught up with us. I was happy to see her and thought that two baskets could hold more than one — this way the *hendshe* would get more to eat. But I said nothing and only walked as fast as I could so as not to fall behind. Mother broke her silence only once to give a menacing order for Arsylang to go home, which he obeyed immediately.

We walked toward Saryg Göschge, discovering along the way little piles of horse droppings that looked dark and so could probably still be used as feed. But the droppings were frozen rock-solid, and lumps of snow, rock, and dirt stuck to them. Separating the droppings from these lumps was hard work.

In the deep hollow of Saryg Göschge, we were protected from the wind. At first we found enough *düüleesh* to quickly fill our baskets, but then we had a hard time. Walking into the wind was almost impossible. Several times we stopped to rest. The resting itself was glorious: We turned our backs to the wind, dropped to the ground, and sat in the shadow of the filled baskets, panting and with our eyes closed, but fully aware that, for the time being, we did not have to fight the wind.

Back home, I cut the soft, grassy tops off the *düül-eesh* and chopped them. While I was busy chopping, Mother melted the horse droppings over the fire. Then she mixed the *düüleesh* and the horse droppings in a bowl and added salt. She took a handful of salt from its bag, sprinkled it over the steaming, tangy mass, and said: "May we drink water rather than let the voracious pack perish!" We called everything that was eaten without salt water. Salt was very valuable and always in short supply.

The *hendshe* wolfed down what we put in front of it. "So," Mother said solemnly, "it's up to us to keep them alive."

Unfortunately, Mother was wrong. Or maybe she was right, and we simply proved not to be up to it. For this is what happened. In the evening, Father came home with the big flock and reported that four lambs had frozen to death on the pasture, and that several more were close to dying. All he had been able to do was to skin the dead animals—which he had to do because of the wool quota—and as he did so, he noticed that they had a bit of fat left on the breast.

The next morning all the sheep that had nearly frozen to death the previous day were added to the little flock. There were many! Together Mother and I went off with this new flock, taking our baskets with us. We went back to Saryg Göschge, where we pulled *düüleesh* and picked up fresh horse droppings while we watched the flock. The cold continued, as did the storm. One lamb died. It was one of mine, the second-crop lamb of the middle one of my three stumpy-eared Blackface ewes. These ewes were sisters and so alike one might have taken them for triplets, but we distinguished them by age. The oldest sister was no longer alive. Pressed by Father, I had given her up for slaughter last winter. Now there was another gap in the family.

We didn't notice until the lamb already lay there dead. If we had noticed earlier, when it stumbled or even when it fell, we might have been able to save it. But we were too late. I drew my knife from the sheath on my belt and started to cut into the dead lamb's belly even before Mother had said anything. Because of the cold it was extremely hard work. My hands got cold, first the left one with which I stretched tight the frost-covered fleece, and later the right one, which I clenched to a fist and shoved between the skin and the body, where it stayed warm as long as it was close to the flesh but then got cold as well.

Mother said we should have paid more attention, and we did from then on. But nothing like that happened again. Heavily loaded down, we drove the flock ahead of us as we returned home in the evening. Once home, we immediately started to prepare more feed.

The big flock had suffered more losses, and again the next morning more animals—this time even fully grown ones—were added to the small flock. Again the two of us went off with our baskets, and again it was the same drudgery.

As the days passed, the flock wasted away in spite of our efforts. There were losses in both flocks. Each morning we lugged away several dead animals, and Father and I skinned them together. By then I had mastered the skill much better. The skins were stretched and frozen, then piled on top of each other next to a rock a little farther away. Later we wet the flesh side of each skin repeatedly and then covered them tightly. Eventually, when they began to rot, we pulled off the wool. The pile grew quickly. The skinned bodies were stored behind the hulking flat rocks that stuck out from the ground below the *hürde* like the remains of a beheaded forest. Arsylang helped carry them over, and then left them to lie there without ever touching them again. Once I cut off the fatty tail of a lamb that had had some strength left and Arsylang, after sniffing it undecidedly for a few moments, wolfed it down in a single gulp. From then on I always gave Arsylang the piece of a carcass that I thought was best: in addition to the fatty tail or meat from the haunches, I also gave him the liver.

Father and Mother were soon showing signs of the strain. Their faces had turned black. Their cheekbones jutted out, and their noses seemed strangely big. I must have been getting emaciated, too, for my whole body felt dead tired, my feet slid around in my boots, and the basket I had to carry seemed to grow heavier by the day.

We rose at dawn and didn't get to bed until the dark of night. Often Father had to get up a few times to check on the flocks. Since the beginning of time, a shepherd who spends his day outside with his sheep has never eaten more than twice a day—early in the morning and late at night. We had always followed this custom, but we always had good meals and enjoyed the companionship that came with them. Now there was no longer time for that. Hardly back on our feet, we would rush out to help the trembling animals that had been lashed by the night's cold. Eating became less important. It was good that we had dried curd cheese: In the morning each of us put a handful of pieces into a breast pocket, and most of the time we kept a piece in our mouth and sucked it. Curd cheese helped stave off hunger as well as thirst. Sometimes at night, when I took off my clothes and untied my belt, a forgotten piece fell out of my coat folds. The cheese always felt warm, soft, and oily to the touch.

With each passing day, the animals grew thinner and thinner, and the flock smaller and smaller. The cold and the storm continued. Then the birthing began. Each morning we checked the flock. Animals whose bellies had dropped and looked sunken were separated out and left in the *hürde*. Sometimes we had to finger their udders. Full, warm udders and reddish teats were a sure sign the ewe would lamb soon. In spite of our checks, Father came home most evenings with his felt bag full and heavy with new-born lambs.

Because she had to look after the lambing ewes and their new-borns, Mother was no longer able to watch the second flock with me. I wanted to continue taking the basket, but Father and Mother would not let me since they were afraid I might stumble in the storm and get choked by the basket sling. So I gathered *düüleesh* and horse droppings into piles instead, and now and then Mother came to pick them up.

Almost every day I had to skin dead animals. It was very hard with the fully grown sheep. They were emaciated, and their skin clung tight. One day in desperate straits I invented an easier process for myself: while pulling and tightening the skin with my left hand, I pounded it with the glow stone in my right hand. Normally, we skinned only large animals that way. Soon I refined the process: I told Arsylang to bite into the skin and pull it tight, which he quickly understood and carried out with great dedication. Now I was able to pound the tightened skin with the stone and then, when my arm got tired, stomp on it with my foot, which was, however, not quite as effective.

During those storm-tossed days I taught Arsylang another trick. One evening yet another animal had died on the way home. I lugged it along until I ran out of strength and had to leave it behind. This was not supposed to happen. During the night it would freeze rock-solid, and that would destroy the valuable wool that Father's life depended on. His head would roll, as he put it. Worried, I realized Arsylang might be able to carry the animal. I pointed at the dead sheep and said: "Arsylang, fetch!" He bit into the shaggy fleece. I lifted and heaved it on his neck, and Arsylang started to walk. He was strong. Every child was familiar with the saying: "Dogs get lucky during the *dshut*, and lamas during the plague." Although it wasn't my four-legged companion's fault, it was true in our case.

In those days the emaciated ewes had little if any milk. Their udders sagged like empty bags, and their teats were cold and lifeless. The lambs bleated with hunger and licked and sucked whatever got in front of their little mouths—other lambs, their mothers' shaggy strands of wool, people's fingers or the seams of their clothes. Mother prepared a gruel of flour, but-ter, herb tea, and salt, to which she sometimes added a bit of milk. Flour was a rarity we only got to taste on holidays. And the milk was drawn one drip at a time from the odd ewe that was a little better off than the others—in the eyes of the mother and her baby, it must have felt like theft. With this gruel we fed the starving lambs. But the hollow sucking sound of the empty horn-bottle betrayed the lambs' persistent hunger. This was not about what you might have called "stilling their hunger" or making them "feel full," it was about getting them to survive the day and endure into the next which might, perhaps, be better. Sometimes I got a little bowl of gruel myself. Then I swore that in the future, when the good times would come, I'd eat nothing but gruel.

Some ewes even rejected their lambs. That happened in other years, too, but now it spread like a devastating infectious disease. When they were supposed to be nursing, we would squat behind these ewes, cling to their udders, and sing for dear life. Yes, we sang! It was not the lyrics that mattered, but the melody, the rich voice, and the repetition: toega— toega—toega ... Sometimes, though, little rhymes would also slip off our tongue:

> If you don't love your little one—
> toega—toega—toega
> You are such a wicked one—
> toega—toega—toega
> If you nurse it all you can—
> toega—toega—toega
> You'll become an Ardshupan—
> toega—toega—toega!

Ardshupan was the hero of the fairy tales I made up and told Arsylang. Ar- came from Arsylang, dshu-

from one of my own names, Dshurukuwaa, and -pan
was meant to indicate great courage.

Father sang:

> As long as we have you—
>   toega—toega—toega
> We are the richest of all—
>   toega—toega—toega
> As soon as we lose you—
>   toega—toega—toega
> We are the poorest of all—
>   toega—toega—toega!

Whom did he have in mind? Hardly those stupid
sheep who left their children to die in order to save
their own meager lives! Maybe he meant the mountains. That was more likely. The mountains protected
animals and people from the wind and the cold and gave
us so much: grass and herbs, bulbs and roots against
the hunger, water and snow against the thirst, *desgen*
and *düüleesh* against the cold. As I thought about it, I
myself suddenly felt like praising the mountains, our
Black Mountains. But first I had to finish telling the
stupid sheep what was most important: If you nurse
your little lamb all you can, you'll become an Ardshupan; if you do not love your little one, remember that
slaughter will come!

Mother, for her part, appealed to the milk, to the white, warm milk. The whole time she repeated the same song:

> Flow, flow milk—
> > toega—toega—toega
> White, white milk—
> > toega—toega—toega
> Hot, hot milk—
> > toega—toega—toega
> Pour, pour milk—
> > toega—toega—toega.

Of course we also tried other means. We brushed highly concentrated brine on the animal baby's bottom and forced the mother's mouth into the saline wool so that the mother, no matter how much she resisted at first, could not help but lick her wet lips, and discover that she liked it. In fact, once she had licked the brine on her lips, she could no longer stop licking until all the taste of salt seemed to be gone. Then we could see which was stronger, her cravings or her stubbornness. If the former won out, she would come back on her own for another sampling of the tasty treat we had prepared for her. Once that happened, all was well. But often her stubbornness won. Then we resorted to our next trick, which was to push several fingers into the ewe's vagina, straighten and bend them in there, and then wipe those fingers on the wool of the lamb's back. How many fingers to use and how far to bend them depended on the ewe's re-action. Where one ewe was responsive, the next one was like a piece of rock. But these were remedies that only the grown-ups used anyhow. I knew about them and watched when they were applied, but so far I had stuck to my singing. My high, clear voice usually took effect on the animals more quickly than the voices of the grown-ups.

In the evenings we stayed late at the *hürde*. If the night was clear, the stars' bluish-yellow light would fall from the sky and bounce off the flock's back. In the shimmering starlight we remained glued to the sheep udders and continued to sing. Darkness lurked all around us, and out of this darkness chills rolled over us in unending waves, which always left behind a yawn. We tried hard to repress this urge, tried to shake it off, but each of us felt the need to drop on the spot and fall asleep instantly among the sheep. We had to keep singing and through our singing, drive the ice from the ewes' bodies, thereby laying bare and re-awakening their feelings of love.

One night Mother appealed to the blue sky. Clouds had sprung up, the storm had died down, the air smelled of snow, and darkness weighed, dumb and heavy, on yurt and *hürde*, people and sheep.

If you still have eyes—
    toega—toega—toega
See me, oh *Deedis*—
    toega—toega—toega
If you still have ears—
    toega—toega—toega
Hear me, oh *Deedis*—
    toega—toega—toega.

Tears began to well up in her voice.

Why this, why, why—
    toega—toega—toega . . .

The tears arrived. The singing broke off, and gave way to sniffling and heaving. I was aware of what was happening next to me, but I continued to sing. Father, too, sang on. He was describing the baby for its animal mother:

Soft little ears—
    toega—toega—toega
Small little mouth—
    toega—toega—toega
Skinny little legs—
    toega—toega—toega
Curly little tail—
    toega—toega—toega

Mother had regained control. Her voice sounded strong again and seemed rested:

You are our father—
toega—toe . . .

But the singing halted abruptly when a scream rang out. The scream began bright and clear, but quickly drowned in muffled, endless gurgling. Eventually the gurgling ebbed into sobs and wheezes. I saw the ewe for whom the disrupted song was meant walk away, and then I saw its lamb fall: the lamb's mother had pushed her baby over as she tore away. The lamb cried and flailed about, but its crying was as faint and weak as its flailing. Mother's sobbing and wheezing, on the other hand, was loud, and I had the feeling that the entire *hürde* was listening and waiting anxiously for what might come next. Words came next—they poured out, one on top of the other, all aimed at the sky. It was as if Mother had grabbed the sky, as if she had grabbed this hard-hearted old father by his hair and was plucking away at him. I was relieved because the wordless sobbing and wheezing had been terrifying.

"Oh, what a hard-hearted father you are!" she yelled, her eyes turned upward. She waved her hands, which were clenched into fists.

"You who punishes us so severely! Oh, what have we done? Have we not lived in constant fear and infinite awe of you? Ah? Why do you punish us so cruelly and needlessly? Eeh? We'd be better off renouncing you and listening to others, we'd be better off turning our backs on you!"

And on it went. It was as if somebody had hurt her deeply and now she was quarreling with him.

Father and I stayed with our sheep, continued our work, kept on singing. I tried to come up with beautiful, difficult words for my song so I wouldn't have to listen to what Mother yelled or rather screamed at the blackish-blue night sky. But the words I needed seemed to hide behind the sheep, and I could not find them. While I relaxed a little even as I searched desperately for words to fill the lines of the toega, I listened and watched helplessly what was happening next to me. I had to admit that Mother was not entirely wrong with her outburst. Father, meanwhile, was endlessly repeating his song about the little ears and the little mouth and the little legs and the little tail. Maybe he felt the same way I did?

Time passed, and Mother must have had second thoughts. Her threats gave way to pleas. In the end she got up and went to look for the ewe that had escaped from her. She was staggering. I would have liked not to have seen her stagger, but I couldn't take my eyes off her.

That night was long and filled with struggle. The sheep were obstinate. The clouds were sinking lower and lower. The world turned as dark and as narrow as if we were stuck in a hole. And all was silent. I felt as if we had been abandoned with the stupid, stubborn sheep, condemned to sing forever in an empty, dark world.

The following night snow fell as expected. But we had not expected the sun that afterward shone on the snow-covered world. Already in the morning the snow began to melt on the southern slopes of the cliffs. Delicate, dark edges appeared around the rags of snow on the blue rock, spread, and eventually touched. "Any wind now, and we'll be done for!" Father said, his voice breaking. Mother cowered and whispered a prayer, her eyes turned to the sky. There were fear and remorse in her eyes.

But the wind never came. The sun continued to burn almost as if it were summer. A bluish light first hung above the snow, then sank down and became one with it. The air simmered. Here and there tiny rills appeared along the southern slopes and grew by the hour. We stood speechless with surprise, anticipation, and hope, taking it all in. Toward evening, mountain and steppe were a checkered black. Two more sunny days with no wind, and there would be no snow left on the slopes facing the sun.

Tracks began to appear in the snow. Mice, rabbits, foxes, stone martens, wild cats, and wolves had run across it in all directions. The tracks were fresh, but not a living thing could be seen. How odd!

Arsylang sniffed them and rushed ahead, his senses alert. Whenever he hit upon wolf tracks, he barked and growled, and sometimes scraped the snow with his back paws, tossed it in the air, and urinated with excitement. There weren't that many wolf tracks, but they were the largest, as the sharp wolf claws had pierced the fresh snow. Somewhere I had heard that in years rich with snow, wild animals grow strong claws and hooves.

Whenever Arsylang got excited, I did too. I would look hard in the direction of the tracks and try to spot the animal that had left them. But I never did.

I wished a stone marten were close by or a fox, or even a wolf—yes, ideally a wolf. Then Arsylang would tear after it and, naturally, catch it. I had no doubt that Arsylang had not only the courage, but also the speed and the strength to defeat any enemy whatsoever. Wouldn't that be something! How I would tell Brother and Sister! And in the summer I would get to tell the other *ail* children as well. My Arsylang would become as famous as Gysyl Galdar, Hüreldej the Warrior's legendary dog. Even the grown-ups would say: "Schynykbaj's youngest, what a great guy he is with his dog Arsylang!"

Could my flock still be called a *hendshe*? Few of the late-born lambs were left, and those whose life blood still pulsed had suffered so much. They were drained and beaten and barely able to stay on their feet. And

yet we could tell that the tottery and wobbly crea-
tures still had their will to live, as they scratched in
the snow for tiny blades of grass. Their will encouraged all of us and strengthened our hope that, maybe,
the wind would stay away altogether. Father was in a
confident mood. His face had brightened during the
course of the day. "Everything points to the *dshut* finally being over," he said, smiling as he drank his milkless, steaming-hot tea.

He, too, had seen tracks, wolf and fox tracks mostly.
And what was more, he was getting into the mood for
a little hunting. Father was a good or rather a first-rate
herder, but a poor hunter. He had never been able to
fill his hunting quota for wolves and foxes. He bought
pelts from other people instead and paid for them with
sheep: a wolf pelt was worth three sheep, a fox pelt
two. And he had a terrible time coming up with the
required five rock partridges and ten gray partridges
since he hardly ever shot any and caught them in a trap
instead. Each year it was the same story, and when the
hunters arrived with their pelts and drove away our
sheep, Mother got angry with him. Father did have a
good rifle, a Mauser, and sometimes he carried it along
with him, but he shot nothing but marmots and even
those not that often. Many of the good hunters poked
fun at him.

Now he wanted to hunt, and he wanted to do it
with poison. Poison was the latest thing. The white

powder looked like today's table salt, and you could find it by the bagful in the yurts; people bought it in the store for roughly the same price as salt. It was called wolf poison, but people used it for whatever they wished to see dead: birds that stole the curd cheese spread out to dry; rodents that dared to get close to the yurt; game whose pelts people needed but whose meat they didn't relish. Eventually, the poison was declared illegal and no longer sold in public, and whoever had any left was asked to turn it in so it could be destroyed. But that didn't happen until we had our first outbreak of rabies.

But in the spring of that year, the novelty had only just arrived and not yet revealed its dangers. It was still surrounded by the brilliance the manufacturer had attached to it by way of a boastful leaflet, which had the gullible nomads under its spell.

So Father melted some butter, poured it into the small intestines from a sheep, and put the sausage outside on top of the yurt for a short time. When it was frozen solid, he cut it into two-finger thick slices, scraped a little hollow into each slice, and used the little silver spoon at the end of his snuff-bottle stopper to stuff the hollows with poison. Each slice got a little spoonful of poison and was sealed with the butter he had scraped out before. The slices—thirty altogether—looked colorful and playful.

When he was done, Father washed his hands and

the little spoon—he even used warm water—and told us about Schirning. Old Man Schirning had passed out and collapsed when he took snuff after having prepared poison-butter slices and only wiping his little snuff spoon when he really should have rinsed it. I knew the old man and called him *Eshej*, like any man older than Father, but mostly he was called Schirning-baj because he was rich and had a dark-brown, quilted velvet coat and a mustache that covered half his face with its twirled and trimmed tips. It made me giggle to think that this man had fainted. But I could hear Mother cry, "Ihiij," the way she always did when she was afraid. "Ihiij," she cried again, "then don't do it— who knows what'll happen."

"Don't worry, I'm always careful," Father interrupted her. Then he added, "Maybe *Deedis* will bring me more luck this way than with the gun and the trap."

Mother didn't reply, but she did look at Father, and for a brief moment her face lit up. Maybe Father would indeed get lucky on the hunt. Who was to know? If he did, the little flock we lost each year because of the hunting quota could remain in our larger flock. We needed them badly. And maybe even more wolves and foxes than we owed the state would bite into a poisoned slice and drop dead. Then we could exchange the extra ones for sheep and goats and whatever else we needed. After all, why couldn't we do what the others did?

We needed three more animals to make up our quota, and Father took thirty poisoned slices with him. Wolves and foxes were said to have a keen sense of smell, which would now lead them to their death— ha! It was another calm day. The sun confidently went about his task, rising and warming the earth after it had cooled down once more the night before.

The *hendshe* struggled with the ice that had formed along some of the edges of the snow islands, but these poor four-legged inhabitants of the earth went to task with the same confidence as the sun in the sky. They hurried onward with their necks craned and their limbs stretched, searching for tiny blades of grass on the rocky, blue ground, and did not shy from scraping the snow even though it was harder than the day before and had formed a thin crust that, quietly clinking, broke beneath their hooves.

Soon, very soon, the ice melted, and the ground began to steam. Rills appeared and by afternoon had become brooks and puddles. The mountains and the steppe glistened. No longer willing to eat *düüleesh*, the *hendshe* wanted real grass and the cool mugwort that had suddenly turned up. I saw that it already grew in places, and its savory scent drifted toward me from all sides.

The animal tracks were fading: increasingly mean-ingless and bluish, they sprawled across the rags of snow. Arsylang sniffed them all as eagerly as the day before, and was no less excited by the remaining wolf tracks. I thought about the wolves even more than before, but now imagined them all dead. The thirty poisoned slices that Father had taken and would have laid out by now occupied my thoughts. They would be spread all over in order to ambush their victims. Shaped into a perfect circle and reddish yellow in color, every one of them looked like the sun. The thirty little suns made me feel hot inside. Maybe the first wolves and foxes were already dead?! Oh, it was such a long day.

In the evening I set out to meet Father. I had waited and waited and finally got through the long yellow spring day, but now I was running out of patience. From afar I tried to make out whether Father was dragging any wolves or foxes. No, both his hands were empty. But I didn't allow myself to get disappointed quite yet. It struck me that he would have skinned any wolf or fox he caught right away. And if he had, their pelts would have been hanging behind him from his belt. I had seen quite a few hunters carry pelts that way. But Father didn't seem to have any pelts dangling behind him. Then I noticed that his felt bag was full. So they were in there! Or were they? My heart was in my mouth when I reached him. "What's in your bag, Father?"

"Lambs. Three lambs. One's got stumpy ears and snow-white skin." I was deeply disappointed. Suddenly weary, I thought: Get lost with your stupid lambs!

But I still did not want to lose hope and asked: "How was the hunt?" I had really wanted to ask where his kill was, but I didn't have the courage. Father understood and said: "I've only just put out the poison today."

"And when are you going to check?"

"Tomorrow, the day after tomorrow. Every day."

I was feeling better.

"The sheep ate their fill today," Father told Mother, beaming with joy. "You'll see." She agreed: "The udders have milk."

We had less work to do than the two previous evenings even though we still stayed out in the *hürde*, still sang till our voices were hoarse, and still crouched, yawning, in the light of the stars.

It was the sixth day of the second month of spring. A full month had passed since the first snow ushered in the *dshut*. "Tomorrow's the make-or-break day," Father said, looking at the sky. He sounded and looked confident. And he was right. The weather stayed mild, and the late spring continued.

That night my dreams were heavy. The last dream was the one I had dreamed once before, a long time ago, the bad one. It had somewhat changed, but I still recognized it: Blue snow has fallen everywhere, beyond the mountain peaks and to the ends of the steppe, wherever the eye can see. I am trying to get out of the snow because I think snow that blue cannot be good. But I can't tell if I am making any progress because the snow is mute. It makes no sound no matter how much I stamp in it. I sense a restlessness growing inside me, and then it turns into fear. I want to scream, but am shocked to find that I have no voice. Suddenly, Arsylang, Grandma, and our flock appear. And my fear does not subside. Instead, it becomes even more unbearable as I notice that they are different from what they were before: they don't walk or run but rather float, and they too are mute. Arsylang barks and howls, the *hendshe* bleats, and Grandma talks. I can see them do it, but I cannot hear a sound. Everybody is mute.

Then I notice that Grandma's face is pale, that her hands are emaciated, and that she has grown very old. The flock consists of nothing but dead animals. And Arsylang has a fixed stare and stiff limbs; he falls over, gets up again, and stumbles. I can tell that he is suffering terribly and wants to bark and howl, but he can't. Then suddenly I hear barking and clip-clopping.

I woke up and heard Arsylang tear off with a muffled bark. Outside, Father was shouting: "Tuh-tuh-tuh!"

"What's up?" I called and jumped up. And then again, since there was no answer: "What's up, Father?"

"A fox."

"Oh."

I hastily slipped into my boots, threw on my *ton*, and dashed to the door. I couldn't see a fox, but I saw Arsylang briefly before he disappeared behind the mountain saddle above the sacrificial cairn. Then there was no more barking.

Although it was still early in the day, Father and Mother were already at work with the sheep. They had let me sleep in. I put on my clothes, tucked a lamb under each arm like a grown-up, and hurried out to help them. The *hürde* seemed to be spilling over with the din of the sheep and lambs, but for a fraction of a second it was as if behind all the noise I could catch the silence of the early-morning earth. It was a strange sight: There was the sun, a garish red, glued to the craggy peaks, while there was still a breath of darkness below, and up above, there was the sky, shining bright. So sharp was the contrast between earth and sky that I couldn't help but feel as if I was standing between day and night. I was aware of the beauty, but my senses quickly turned in the direction the dog and the fox had likely gone. I was waiting for Arsylang's return. And while I waited, I thought about my dream. It was a bad dream. I needed to tell it to a hole in the ground and spit three times. I should have done so earlier, when I went to relieve myself. Now I was stuck with my work and was stared at and bleated at from all sides. I couldn't simply leave the stupid, impatient lambs and sheep that were following each and every one of my movements to dash off and rid myself of my dream. For the time being, I would have to lug it along with me.

With each chunk of time that passed, the dream weighed more and more heavily on me. Finally the *hürde* was empty, and the lambs were grazing. But Arsylang did not come.

Only a few sheep mothers were left to listen to our singing. The songs were short, but I found it difficult to sing. Arsylang did not come.

The lambs that had drunk their fill were caught again. The youngest ones were brought back into the yurt, while those who were already able to graze were sent into the *hendshe's* sheepfold.

Arsylang did not come.

I was told to have breakfast. The tea wasn't too hot or too tepid, but I had only one bowl full and ate nothing, although I did put a handful of curd cheese into my breast pocket as usual.

Arsylang did not come.

Mother asked if maybe he had in fact come back. I said he had not. Father was about to say something but stopped himself and noisily slurped tea from his colorful yellow china bowl.

"It's odd," he said finally.

The big flock was about to leave the *hürde*. I opened the gate to let the sheep out. The flock had grown and become more sightly again, thanks to the white fleeces of the lambs. The young ones who were leaving for pasture for the first time tried to run back to the *hürde*. I chased after them, every so often looking in the direction from which Arsylang should have come. But he still did not come.

As soon as I had got away from the yurt, I took on a solemn posture, raised my eyes to look across the steppe, and lightly stretched my arms out in front of me with my palms turned up. Then I told the dream and spat three times. Once I had completed this task and shifted the burden of the dream off myself, I felt some small relief.

The rays of the sun felt as hot and sharp as in summer. A slight, fragrant breeze passed over me, vanished, and a little later made its presence felt again. It smelled of new growth, although the eye could see no trace of green yet. Sparkling like a shard of glacier, a lark was flung out of the blue and hovered in the air at the height of a lasso's length, fluttering its wings. I wished it would sing, but it was mute.

The lambs baaed and gamboled. Now and again they got startled and jumped apart with breezy drumming, then piled again into a ball, and soon started the noisy game all over. Their older brothers, the *hendshe*, did not much care for the game; they searched single-mindedly for blades of grass and found a few.

What was it Grandma had always said? Bird songs ward off disaster, while bird screams bring it about. Brother Galkaan once claimed he had found out first-hand that she was right. Sister Torlaa had had a good laugh at him. She figured screams were like songs. Only now did I realize how little I had thought of Brother and Sister recently, and I felt ashamed. But I noticed that my shame quickly became a burning, smarting desire to see Brother and Sister and to have them with me that very moment so I could share with them the beauty of spring.

Then I wished that Grandma, too, could be with me. If only she would be standing in front of the yurt with that child's smile in her wrinkled, kindly face when I got home, or when the three of us came home like three *yrgaj* branches. I had never seen a *yrgaj*, but I knew that it was a tree and that everybody with good fortune in life got to see it once. Grandma had told me as much, and it was she, too, who had said to the three of us: "May you grow tall and strong, and may you stick with each other like three *yrgaj* branches!" A gift had preceded that blessing: the ewe Dshojtung had given birth to triplets, and Grandma had given each of us a lamb. But none of the triplets was left. The last of the three, Üshüsbej, belonged to Sister Torlaa before it died during the last *dshut*. The triplets were no longer alive, and the three of us who were to stick with each other had been separated. Why? Grandma alone would have known. It was time she came back from the salt, or from whatever it was that existed forever. If only Grandma would come back!

All that longing and remembering sharpened my senses as I became even more aware that Arsylang had not come back. For the first time ever I thought that an accident might have befallen him. The thought alone made me cry, but instead of wiping away my tears or holding back new ones, I began to pray. "Oh *Deedis*, oh my rich Altai!" I exclaimed and lifted my arms. I was speaking even as I was weeping floods of tears. "Please hear me and stand by me: Where is my Arsylang? Oh dear, dear *Deedis*! Please, please let him be safe! And stave off any accident that might lie in ambush for him." Then I began to sob and could not go on. If only it would pass! I imagined how Arsylang, had he been with me, would have squatted beside me and howled to the sky and to all four corners of the earth. I was shaken by the thought and suddenly sensed a lump inside me that seemed to be growing bigger and heavier. Pain was radiating out from it, so much pain that it almost made me faint. I cried out again and again. Later I no longer felt the pain. But then I was afraid that it might come back, and I clenched my teeth and tried to choke back my tears and sobs.

The attack passed. But my restlessness stayed, and gradually solidified into certainty: Something had happened to Arsylang.

I worried about all sorts of dangers. A fox never could have harmed him. Arsylang could handle not just a fox but even a wolf. But what if a fox had lured him to a pack of wolves? His only salvation would have been to turn around immediately and flee from the pack. Would Arsylang have done that? Hardly. He would have put up a fight.

On the other hand, he might have stepped into a trap. Admittedly, I hadn't heard anything about Father setting traps again, but who knew; maybe he had. Or perhaps Arsylang had stumbled upon a forgotten trap. Somebody could have set it, covered it with dried, pulverized dung, sprinkled a thin layer of sand on top, and no one would have known what lay underneath. If later on the hunter lost his way and could no longer find his trap, he would have told himself that a wolf or bear had stepped into it and dragged the trap away, when in fact it could have lain there for a year, or for two years, or five . . . until finally someone stepped on the ground that was hiding such danger—and this someone was Arsylang!

Or perhaps—this took my breath away and almost made me sick. I tried to think of some other possibility but failed. Arsylang was not a horse, which might throw itself off a rock. Nor was he a sheep that might stumble into a crevice and break a leg—even with a broken leg he would have been able to drag himself home. No, no, everything else was out of the question.

I decided to look for him. But first I pointed the *hendshe* toward the *hürde* and hollered a few threats over to the odd lamb that tried to turn back. Then I went, or rather ran, up toward the bright path that lay far above me like a ring around the mountain's chest. It was a steep climb, but I kept running, and kept falling, on the slippery slate gravel. Hurrying along, I prayed silently to everything around me: to the sky that swayed and shimmered above the path and the rocky ridge, to the stony steep slope I was battling my way up, to the mountain high above me and to the next one beyond it, to all of the mountains. I pleaded with them to protect my Arsylang.

Finally I reached the path. It no longer resembled a ring, but rather a scarred-over wound that seemed to have gnawed its way into the earth and its rocks, into the mountain's body. I reached the path and stumbled. For a moment I stayed on my knees in the dusty, ringing gravel, fingering a bare rock that poked through the ground and had been polished in the course of time by feet, hooves, and paws, and by wind and water. I could suddenly hear myself panting, feel myself sweating, and sense a burning behind my chest bone. But I got back on my feet and rushed on. Now it was easier. Now I was racing and had more strength to pray. I prayed to the sky, which had turned reddish and brilliant. I prayed to the breezes that filled the sky and to the winds and the clouds which, though invisible, had to be there, at rest after finishing their work high above all living beings below. I prayed to the mountain saddle Ak Gertik, which was coming toward me, to all the saddles, hills, and peaks, and to all the hollows, valleys, and gorges beyond it, naming each in due order: Saryg Gertik, Gök Gertik, Hara Gertik, Dsher Haja, Myshyktalyyr, Gongaadaj, Dsher Aksy, Dshukschud . . . I prayed to the path I was treading, the path my forebears and their herds had already tread, addressing it as the great wide path that was part of all paths leading to the three worlds and their thirty-three oceans—phrases I had learned by listening to Father. I prayed and prayed for Arsylang. For my Arsylang.

I found him at the lower end of the Myshyktalyyr gorge. Tall and dark, he faced me but stood unsteadily like a young yak suffering from brain disease. Then he reeled back. A few steps behind him was the edge of the mountain. A steep rock face dropped into the dreaded abyss that plunged several rifle shots deep before bottoming out in the great river that carried off the waters of all Tuvan rivers.

I wanted to let out a cry, to call the dog by his name, but I couldn't: I had fallen mute. Instead I tore down the steep slope. With each step I leapt and fell and bounced off the ground like a stone that has sprung from the slope and free-falls down the mountainside. I managed to control my tumbling body just in time to stop before Arsylang. And then I touched him.

He was unrecognizable. His hair stood on end, which made him seem tall and dark. His limbs were spread and stiff, his head was thrown back, and his muzzle covered with froth. His eyes had taken on a reddish shine and were fixed in a vacuous stare, while the gaping pupils were terrifyingly alive and glowed like two holes blazing with raging fires. He trembled and gasped and seemed to be fighting a force that was pulling him backward. I could tell that he was power-less and losing the ground below his feet one span at a time. Just then he must have recognized me, for he made a little noise that sounded like crying.

I was still under the spell of the muteness that had overwhelmed me farther up on the mountain, and so I was not crying myself even though tears were filling my eyes and blinding me. I grabbed hold of Arsylang as best I could, clutched him against me, trying to grasp what had happened.

Finally my shock gave way and I realized what was happening. I decided to resort to the ultimate: I would turn to the sky himself and plead for help—and ei-ther he would hear me and instantly bestow his help upon me, or I would renounce him forever. This fortu-nate flash of inspiration came from stories I had heard. Such things were talked about in legends. I had never seen or heard any of the people I knew personally try it out though.

So I took off my belt, tied a heavy rock to each end, put the burden around my neck, knelt down, turned my eyes to the sky, and called out: "EH-EH-EEH, *GÖK-DEERI!*"

I was glad that my voice had come back. It sounded eerily loud and multiplied as happens in a gorge. The echoes resounding from the rocks chased and crossed each other in all directions. With shock and awe I listened to that grave word which had never before crossed my lips but which I had uttered right then and which each and every rock was now shouting back at me in my own voice, as if the Altai was hurling it at me from all sides. There was no turning back. Now that I had awakened the Supreme One, I had to tell him why I had done so. So I continued: "HEAR ME, EH-EH-EEH, *GÖK-DEERI*! HOLIEST OF ALL WHO ARE HOLY, GREATEST OF ALL WHO ARE GREAT! THIS IS YOUR SON DSHURUKUWAA, WHOM IN THE YEAR OF THE BLACK HORSE YOU GAVE TO THE SON OF HYLBANG AND HIS WIFE ORLUMAA SCHYNYKBAJ, AND TO THE DAUGHTER OF LOBTSCHAA AND HIS WIFE NAMSYRAA BALSYNG, SO THAT HE MAY CONTINUE THE TRIBE OF IRGID, WHICH HAD ITS BEGINNINGS IN THE WHITE MILK OF THE GRAY WOLF AND IN THE RED BLOOD OF THE BROWN DEER!"

The gorge was filled with my voice. From all sides I could hear myself make a racket and felt quietly satisfied that I had been able to adapt words from a shaman's chant for my purposes. But my smugness vanished instantly when I saw another terrible cramp torment my dog.

"EH-EH-EEH, ETERNAL FATHER OF ALL FATHERS,

SONS, AND GRANDSONS, HEAR ME AND KNOW: I
AM ONE WHO STILL HAS TEETH LIKE NITS AND
HAIR LIKE DOWN, AND WHO HAS AN EYE FULL OF
WATER AND A HEART MADE OF FLESH."

With the last words, self-pity took hold of me and
tears began to well up. I suddenly became aware of the
weight of my rocks. Although I figured this was how it
was meant to be, the rocks were so heavy that I had to
hurry to exclaim the most important part:

"EH-EH-EEH, *GÖK-DEERI*, MOST KNOWLEDGE-
ABLE OF ALL WHO ARE KNOWLEDGEABLE, MOST
POWERFUL OF ALL WHO ARE POWERFUL! HAVE
MERCY UPON YOUR POOR, WEAK CHILD AND LET
MY DOG LIVE! EH-EH-EEH, *GÖK-DEERI*, HEAR ME
AND STAND BY ME! LET MY DOG LIVE! EH-EH-EEH,
GÖK-DEERI, I HAVE CALLED YOU BY YOUR NAME
AND HAVE DARED THE ULTIMATE. NOW I AWAIT
YOUR HELPING HAND AND THAT ONLY: IF YOUR
HELP ARRIVES, I WILL BE YOURS EVEN MORE IN THE
FUTURE THAN I HAVE BEEN IN THE PAST. BUT IF IT
DOES NOT, I WILL NO LONGER BE YOURS, AND YOU
WILL HAVE LOST A SON! FOR EVER AND EVER!"

I could have stopped there. But I felt a remnant of
strength and the need to add the following for the sake
of clarity: "EH-EH-EEH, *GÖK-DEERI*, DEAR AND HOLY
FATHER! LET MY DOG LIVE, MY ARSYLANG, WHO
IS A BROTHER TO ME IN PLACE OF A BROTHER,
A FRIEND IN PLACE OF A FRIEND! LET ME, WHO

LOVES AND WORSHIPS YOU, CONTINUE TO BE A
SON TO YOU!"

I paused and waited. In the epic, help was always
quick to come. The sky sends rain in torrents that hit
the enemy like thunderbolts and wash the wounds of
the hero in need so they will heal in no time. While I
could hardly imagine such a miracle actually coming
about, even less could I imagine it not coming about.
So I stayed patiently on my knees with my arms lifted,
my eyes turned to the sky, and my belt with its two
rocks across my neck. Behind me I could hear Arsylang
gasp and stumble. He had once more moved a bit farther away from me.

I would have dearly loved to turn around, to catch
up with him and hold him fast in order to stop him
from drawing any closer to the edge of the cliff. But
I was waiting for the miracle the sky was bound to
send me. The weight of the burden pulling me to the
ground only increased my defiance. So I crouched on
my knees, grew stiff and stubborn, and waited.

It ended when I broke down. All of a sudden I
fell forward on the sandy gravel. It was good to feel
the solid ground supporting my stiff, numb arms, and
equally good to feel the cool rock touching my hot face.
I threw off my burden, struggled to get up, and rushed
over to Arsylang, who had teetered all the way over
to the edge. When I got to him, the blue void seemed
to reach for me. I could clearly feel my hair stand on

end, and the next moment I felt jerked up into the air. I let out a cry, threw myself backward, and fell on my buttocks. I could not decide whether to open my eyes—which I had closed without intending or even knowing I had done so when I fell backward—but I opened them anyway. I saw Arsylang right in front of me and quickly reached for him, grabbed his neck, and pulled. He was as heavy as a rock, and I realized that I could no longer keep him where he was, let alone pull him close. I sensed a weight that I could not match. Only then did it occur to me that I should have turned Arsylang around earlier so that, being constantly pulled backward, he would have stumbled away from this cliff. I might even have managed to take him home. As it was, I was afraid to get up. The mere idea paralyzed me and hurt me to the roots of my hair. I felt cheated, and I was sorry I had been so rash to take on the sky without knowing beforehand if word about his helpfulness was true. The thought came as a shock. I tried to drive it away and to con-jure up a different thought to prove the sky's om-nipotence and mercy: The rain He sent to earth year after year, almost always at the exact same time— what would have come of us without it? And the sun He gave us each day, and the moon and the stars He gave us each night! Oh, it was good that I instantly had all sorts of evidence at my command. The grave, terrible thought had been suppressed—though not wiped out. Indeed, no thought can ever be wiped out. Now I knew.

Meanwhile I lay flat on my belly as Arsylang slipped away. With each breath, sensation and strength drained from that arm of mine that his life depended on. I realized that one span of ground was all that was left, and I was terrified that it, too, would soon slide from us. Arsylang would slip from my fingers no matter how hard I dug into his coat. I would never see him again, just as I would never see Grandma again. I would be left alone with my flock, which had itself been beset by heavy losses. I would watch for Brother and Sister alone, and I would walk toward them alone when they came home. This would be my future. It had just begun.

My mind told me as much. But at the bottom of my heart I had not accepted these thoughts, nor did I want to. With everything in my power I resisted.

Then another stubborn thought came to mind: What if Arsylang's hindlegs were to step into the abyss and out of sheer terror he'd bite into my sleeve to hang on? Panic overcame me and left me feeling sick. But still, I was not willing to let go of the dog to save myself.

Convulsed with fear, I began to pray in a low voice: "FATHER SKY AND MOTHER EARTH! HEAR ME AND STAND BY ME: GIVE MY ARM THE STRENGTH TO HOLD THIS DOG WHERE HE IS NOW, AND THE

STRENGTH NOT TO LET HIM MOVE A FINGER'S WIDTH FURTHER!" At that moment I heard a shout. It was Father's voice: "Hang on — I'm on the way! Hang on — I'm on the way!"

The miracle! flashed through my mind. I was overcome by gratitude for the sky's mercy, and new tears welled up in my eyes. All the same, I did not forget that I now needed to hold fast even more. And so I did. Meanwhile Father crept toward us, apparently on tiptoe. I missed the moment he reached me and was startled when he grabbed my knees from behind. As I learned later, he had thought the dog was clinging to me with his teeth and wanted to reach us unnoticed.

When he pulled me to him, I screamed: "Not me! Get Arsylang!" He grabbed for Arsylang and seized one of his front paws. Now we were pulling together. Arsylang looked half dead already. His pupils were gaping but empty as if the blaze behind them had burned itself out. His body seemed lifeless when we poked it, and it was beginning to turn stiff. "Ej, for Heaven's sake," Father lashed out. "He must have swallowed some poison. It's too late to do anything about it. Thank goodness the worst hasn't happened to you, my little one!"

I was devastated. Too late to save Arsylang — just when he had been rescued from the abyss? No miracle after all? How stupid to call that good. Stupid and mean! I jumped with pain. Then I pulled myself up hard and yelled at Father: "You have done in my Arsylang, you and your stupid poison! And now you say it's too late to do anything! And you say thank goodness?"

With the last word I mimicked him.

I expected to get my ears boxed. But Father didn't move. I saw him grow pale and his lips tremble. Why didn't he hit me? Why didn't he fling me to the ground with a slap or a kick? Why not? At least then I would have had reason to cry and scream and rage, and try to throw off the pain. But instead I was left at its mercy, not knowing what to do next. We both stood there without moving, as if we were waiting for the end. Waiting for Arsylang to fall over and die. So we could say he was dead. So we could go home. So, once home, we could wash our hands with juniper extract, eat and drink, and go to bed after having struggled with the sheep and their lambs, only to get up and struggle some more with the sheep and their lambs. So, in short, we could get on with life without Arsylang. How awful and how shameful. Father asked why my belt lay there with rocks tied to it. I told him what had happened.

"Oh, my son," Father said sadly, "once the terrible poison gets into the stomach, it's too late. Then not even the sky can help."

I did not reply, I had no reply. I could not grasp it.

Father let go of the gasping and trembling dog he

had held and supported up to this point, walked over to my belt, untied the rocks, came over to me, and put the belt back on me. I did not move. With one hand on Arsylang's flank, I could feel death spreading inside him. With my belt around me I felt a little relief, some slight support. Suddenly I remembered the story of Old Man Schirning and shouted, "Milk! Could milk possibly help?"

Father paused and looked at me. His eyes lit up. I took heart again. "Let's go," Father said. "We'll take him to the flock." With a tug he lifted Arsylang and flung him over his shoulder. We went up the gorge, climbed the steep rockface. I ran, or tried to. Father couldn't run, but he was only a few steps behind.

I was furious to find that the flock was no longer where Father had left it. The animals had wandered toward the *ail* and the *hürde*. Now I ran faster and Father called after me: "Don't wait for me. Run and tell Mother to get some milk." I ran fast. Downhill was easy.

I caught up with the flock by the edge of the *ail*. When I saw the *hürde* and then the yurt, I started to roar: "Ihi-iiij! Ihi-iiij!" Mother was nowhere to be seen, and I was about to explode with rage because she wasn't coming out of the yurt and walking toward me with her milk pail. Suddenly I heard her voice on the other side, over where the small flock was, and saw her hobbling toward me. She was suffering from the pain in one of her legs that would eventually force her to use a cane. "What's up?" she called. "A disaster has happened, a disaster!" I yelled back. I continued to gallop toward the yurt. Luckily, I found a wooden bucket filled with milk in the yurt. I grabbed it and ran back. In the meantime, Mother had made quite a bit of headway, but rather than wait for her to arrive I began to dash back to Father. But Mother called, "Wait for me, will you? Wait!" So I had to stop and wait for her to make it all the way to me. She seemed to take an eternity. I was seething with rage and shouting: "Faster, faster! *Hara mola!*" The latter was a rather harmless curse which many people used in a kindly teasing manner, but in our family it was only used in the most extreme cases. Now I used it on my own mother.

At long last she arrived. "What has happened, *Deedis*?" she asked. She was panting, and her voice shook. "Arsylang has swallowed poison," I cried with tears in my voice because I had lost so much time waiting for her. Again I reached for the bucket.

"And where is Father?"

"On his way, with Arsylang."

As I dashed off, I heard Mother call, "Oh, my rich Altai!" She sounded joyful.

I was offended by her joy. I was offended because Arsylang was perhaps already dead. I tore off and did not respond to what she shouted next.

I found them behind the first mountain saddle. Father gently tried to stand Arsylang on his legs, but the dog was no longer up to it. So we laid him on his side instead. His legs stretched outward as if he was trying to flee from the poison and the death that had already nested in his belly. His tail stood up straight. Although the only sign of life was a quiet rattle, we tried to force milk into him. Since his teeth were clenched, Father stuck the tip of his knife into a gap behind his fangs to pry his jaws open. But the teeth pressed hard against each other and would not be parted. Foaming slime oozed from the gaps, and when we wiped it off, something that was a very dark red, almost black, became visible. It must have been his tongue.

In the end, we stuck an onion stem into one of Arsylang's nostrils and dripped milk into it. I took milk from the pail and into my mouth, and released it into the stem. Father warned me not to get too close to the dog because he had heard that poison can cause rabies.

The milk we cleverly trickled into one nostril soon came out the other one, but what came out was foaming like water and curd.

A racking cramp shot through Arsylang's body. Then he cried, more softly than before. At that moment I noticed Mother. All of a sudden she was standing next to me. Although my grudge against her had not died down, I felt a flash of gratitude. It was the kind of gratitude you feel toward people who have stood by you through some great disaster. I knew then that Arsylang was dying. Still, I was astonished when Father said it was over with the dog—astonished not so much because the death that was already inside Arsylang had now completed itself, but rather because anybody could simply say, "It's over with the dog," as if he were saying, "The milk has gone sour," or "The wooden pail leaks," or "The horseshoe is worn through."

The gratitude I had felt toward Father for staying with me and the dead Arsylang and for not going after one of his countless other jobs clouded over, disappeared, and finally became anger. When I tried to find reasons to blame him, I did not have to look far. Arsylang wasn't just any old dog. There were many dogs around, but Arsylang was the best among them. He was entirely unique, and yet Father had poisoned him! And then another thought flashed through my mind, some dark inkling. Soon a puppy would arrive, get raised, and take Arsylang's place. I held Father responsible for this untimely thought as well, even though it had been me who had thought it. I simply assumed, without a moment's doubt, that he would have had the same idea.

Right then I heard Mother say, "I was so worried about you." To my ears it sounded like, "Lucky it was just the dog!" Instantly my gratitude toward Mother died as well. Something dark and bitter crept over it and spread and hardened into rock.

The world was beyond understanding. I began to feel deathly ill. I had to do something, I had to rear up and shatter the rock inside me and spit it out so it would not kill me the way the poison had killed Arsylang. And so I did. I wrenched myself up, stepped over beside the dead Arsylang, raised my fists to the sky, and screamed, "I-ih-iiij, *Gök-Deeri!*"

It must have shocked my parents terribly, for everything went quiet around me.

"I-ih-iiij, what sort are you if you are so powerless against a pinch of measly powder?"

At that, Father jumped at me, but I fled, my fists raised, and continued to scream: "Have you turned old and deaf and blind? Or are you so evil that you would not deign to hear and help me in my time of need?!"

Father got a hold of me, but I continued to scream: "Yes, it was you! You let it all happen: that Brother and Sister were taken from me, that Grandma died, that the flock was lost, and that my dog is now dead!"

Father held me and tried to silence me: "Let it be, my dear, dear child! Let it be, I ask you, I beg you."

But I would not hear of it: "I-ih-iiij, *Gök-Deeri*, what have I done wrong? What have I done to deserve this? Are you not ashamed to have done all this to a poor, weak child? I-ih-iiij, *gögergen Gök-Deeri*, i-ih-iiij!"

Then Mother was right in front of me. Her eyes wide with horror, she forced my arms down and said something I didn't hear. "E-eh-eej, *Gök-Deeri!* Deaf one who did not hear me, now listen to how I shall punish you—" Mother had put her hand over my mouth, but the force used against me only pushed me to the edge. I became a savage beast, kicking and hitting, scratching and biting, until eventually I escaped Father's grip. And then, waving my clenched fists, I pronounced judgment on *Gök-Deeri*, our blue sky: "From now on, I will no longer be your son. I will have nothing but contempt for you, i-ih-iiij, *gögergen Gök*—"

At that my head was dealt a blow and I lost my voice. It would have been easy to think the sky had struck me—my once powerful, now shabby *Gök-Deeri*—but I knew it was Father who had whacked me. Barely conscious, I sensed myself falling to the ground and tumbling down the stony slope. Then I felt hands on my neck and my face, and I noticed a face above me. It was blurry, but I recognized Mother by her calloused warm hands. She held my neck and stroked my cheeks. A little further up, outlined against the evening sky, I noticed another tall, blurry figure. I instantly picked up the fight again which, at that moment, seemed to me a fight I was neither allowed to quit nor to put off. I roughly pushed away Mother's hands, got up, staggered toward the figure, and roared with all my strength: "I-ih-iiij, now that you have poisoned my dog, why don't you kill me, too! Go right ahead and kill me, I am ready! Why should I continue to struggle on this earth, far from Brother and Sister, without Grandma, without my flock and without Arsylang, beneath a sky that is blind and deaf?!"

Suddenly all the troubles and sacrifices I had endured during the endlessly long spring came back to me, and words poured out of me like water gushing from a turned-over basin: "Beat me to death or finish me off some other way. If you think I am afraid of dying, you are wrong. If you don't kill me, I'll do it myself. I'll jump off a cliff or do myself in some other way. I want to die, and I want to be eaten by black worms. I am not your child anyway, I am your slave. Have you ever let me sleep in? Do you even know how cold I am, how hungry, and how tired? All you ever think of are your animals. Fodder for the wolves! You never think of your children! You have already given away two of them. And as for me, you make me slave away like a Kazakh herdboy!"

I hurled these words the way people hurl rocks. I wanted them to hit my parents, to hurt and kill them.

"I want to die and be eaten by black worms, i-ih-iiij! Die and be done with, like others before me. I want to go where Grandma went: into death, i-ih-iiij! Do you really think I still don't know? Grandma is dead, and you got rid of her like a dead sheep or a dead cat. You have probably hidden her under some gravel or in a hole in the ground. Or maybe you threw her to the foxes and the wolves. You keep talking about a journey and about the salt, but I know what is going on. You're lying through your teeth because you think I am a fool, but I am not!"

By then I could see and hear clearly again. My parents stood as if chased apart and looked past me silently. It was probably this wretched picture that brought me to my senses. I suddenly understood that they hadn't tried to beat me to death, but merely to silence me. And then it dawned on me that I was without Grandma, without Arsylang, without the flock I had once owned, separated from Brother and Sister, at war with the sky, and about to go to war against my parents! I would lose what little I had left. There was no way I could afford to lose them, so I had to resign myself to what had happened.

Someone who was inside me, but could not be me, was saying these things. It must have been a stranger. There was no way I would listen to him. I did not know him; he had only just showed up, alien and disgusting, and was insulting me along with everything that had ever happened, everything that had been part of my life, everything that nobody had the right to tear away from me.

I pulled myself together and resumed the fight. I screeched for all I was worth, lashed out in all directions, threw myself to the ground, jumped up, stumbled again, threw myself down once more, and then jumped up again. What was the point of my birth and my survival? What was the point of my dreams and my prayers? What was the point of the blessings others had given me, of their praise and their promises, or of the efforts I myself had made? I had been cheated out of a life. I did not belong between sky and earth.

So far, my voice hadn't gone hoarse nor my body limp. But I knew I was about to lose my voice and the strength in my limbs, and that thought enraged me more than anything else.

But the same knowledge also made me fight. Who was I if I could not ward off the injustice so shamelessly inflicted upon me?

Why was I this way?

Why was it this way?

Why, i-ih-iiij, why?

The defiance in me blazed fiercely.

Under no circumstances would I give up the fight. I had to fight to the finish, come what may. So what if my neck broke and my thread of life snapped? So what if I bit the dust, forever the poor devil, and black worms ate me? So what if the loaded dice fell that way? And so I went on, ranting and raving . . .

GLOSSARY

Ail (Mongolian) settlement consisting of several yurts

Aimag (Mong.) administrative unit (provinces or regions); in Tuvan, it can refer to any administrative unit

Arate (Mong.) poor herder, a pillar of Socialist society

Awaj (Tuvan) sister, aunt; form of address for females among one's paternal relatives

Baj (Turkic) rich person

Daaj (Tuv.) maternal relatives

Darga (Mong.) supervisor, head, person in position of authority

Deedis (Tuv.) euphemism for *Deeri*—sky

Desgen (Tuv.) plant with a strong, hard root

Dör (Tuv.) the north side of a yurt, opposite the entrance, considered the place of honor

Dshargak (Tuv.) skirt-like piece of clothing made of sheep or goat leather, worn by the poor

Dshelbege (Tuv.) fairy-tale character who devours everything but is never satisfied

Dshele (Tuv.) a rope to tether yak calves and foals

Dshula (Tuv.) a lamp that burns clarified butter, used for religious purposes

Dshut (Tuv.) violent weather, most often leading to a lack of food for the animals

Düüleesh (Tuv.) alpine plant with strong roots and soft, bushy tops

Enej (Tuv.) grandmother

Eshej (Tuv.) grandfather

Gashyk (Tuv.) ankle bones of sheep and goats, used both as a toy and as an oracle

Gök-Deeri (Tuv.) blue sky, revered as sacred

Hara mola (Tuv.) curse, referring to a Kazakh burial marker

Hara-Sojan (Tuv.) one of the three main ethnic groups among the Tuvans, the other two being the *Ak-Sojan* and the *Gök-Mondshak*

Hendshe (Tuv.) baby lambs, kept in a flock by themselves and herded by children; also, the youngest child

Höne (Tuv.) a rope made from yak hair to tether lambs and kids

Hürde (Tuv.) sheepfold or pen made of wickerwork, usually portable

Khalkh (Mong.) largest and dominant ethnicity in Mongolia; its language is Mongolia's official language and the language of Mongolian literature

Kulak (Russian) fist; peasant in Russia wealthy enough to own a farm and hire help; also applied to wealthy Mongolian herders

Örtöö (Mong.) express-messenger mail service, created by Mongolian rulers in the 13th century and abolished only in 1949. The distance between two *Örtöö* was roughly 30 kilometers. *Örtöö* service relied on the unpaid labor of impoverished males and their provision of mounts free of charge

Oshuk (Tuv.) fireplace consisting of iron rings, on four feet

Pidilism (Mong.) colloquial term for feudalism

Sum (Mong.) administrative unit (district or prefecture)

Ton (Tuv.) skirt-like piece of clothing for the cold season

Yak (Tibetan) long-haired cattle breed of the Central Asian mountains

Yrgaj (Tuv.) tamarisk-like shrub; its red, hard wood is used for whip handles

Yurt (Turkic) circular tent of felt, skins, etc., on a collapsible wooden framework; widely used in Central Asia

WORDS TO ACCOMPANY
MY *BLUE SKY* CHILD

Truly I have had enough difficult hours in my life. Yet at different times, and in different places of my life's work, I have called myself blessed, for the life I have been granted has been both long and rich. I say long because inside a single skin and a single lifespan, I have been privileged to experience almost everything that humankind—since the time of Adam, or the apes, if you prefer—has had to go through to rise to its present state. I have been a gatherer, hunter, and herder; a school boy, a university student, and a professor; a trade union journalist, a shadow politician, and quite a few more things. Today I am the chieftain of a tribe, a healer, an author, a father and a grandfather. I know how to slaughter sheep and how to hunt marmots with or without weapons. I know how to skin them, cut up their bodies and prepare their meat in different ways; I know how to tan their pelts and how to cut and sew them into different pieces. I know how to cobble, how to do carpentry, roll felt, set up and take down a yurt, shoe horses and break in their young; I know how to milk goats and mares and how to let their milk ferment to *kumys* and distil it into schnapps; and I know how to support birthing cows as well as women, and much more beyond. During my lifetime, I have lived in an indigenous, feudal, and communist society. Today, I move about the country on horseback, by car, or by plane. With my shaman's whisk, a truncheon, or a laptop, I alternate between living in the indigenous culture of the post-Socialist Tuvans, the rising tribal capitalism of Mongolia, and the enlightened state monopoly of Western Europe. Finally, my life has been rich because I have always found myself at the focal point of each epoch and have pursued all my tasks and each of my professions with passion.

The Blue Sky is the first part of my autobiographical trilogy. It describes my early childhood and ends with my rejection of Father Sky. The second part, *The Gray Earth*, deals with the violence inflicted on me when I underwent a period of re-education in a totalitarian school system. The outlawed art of shamanism competed with the body of knowledge of a modernity under communist rule. Outer violence triggered resistance: I recanted my rejection of Father Sky from the end of the trilogy's first part, and fiercely chose a return to my roots. The trilogy's final part, *The White Mountain*, traces the unavoidable mental breakdown of the adolescent forced to lead a double life. Both of the latter books contain stories more tragic than those in *The Blue Sky*, but since the art of survival is strong among nomads, some primordial serenity hovers above everything. I survived and was preserved for that small, vanishing remainder of my people for whom each member is vital. By the end of the trilogy I arrived in the wider world, and although still a blind human pup, I had already forgotten how to whimper. I thought then that life had tanned me; that the period of my life during which I had been cooked and left to ferment like mare's milk had come to an end. But today I know that each new phase in life brings its own boiling heat with which to get under your skin; its own paralyzing cold; and its own murderous poison—powers none can get past without making the required sacrifices.

I have been one who has hastened with seven-league boots across our planet's racked field of history. One who has been particularly indifferent, even careless, about three things: my career, clothing fashions, and literary trends. Although my views about other things in life have continued to change, my fundamental faith in the indivisibility and immortality of a soulful and spirit-filled universe has, I believe, remained unshakable. Humankind, which for me in the beginning meant my small tribe of Tuvan people, has grown larger and richer in my heart with the addition of other peoples. Now, the publication of *The Blue Sky* extends it for me even further by including the peoples of North America. I am mightily pleased, not least for these peoples themselves, whose world, in turn, will now include the mountain steppe of Central Asia, and whose awareness of humankind will embrace the nomadic people from that corner.

My father was called Schynykbaj, his father Khylbangbaj, and my grandfather's father, Tümenbaj. And if the flow of history in my homeland had not been disrupted but had continued in its familiar bed, my name would have likely been Dshurukbaj. *Baj* denotes in all Turkic languages 'rich,' or 'somebody rich, noble, or powerful.' 'Tümen' in my great-grandfather's name means ten thousand. It was not his original name but an honorific he was given when his herds numbered ten thousand animals. Khylbàngbaj, my grandfather, was not quite as rich, but rich enough—he was still the richest man in the country. His many sheep, goats, horses, and yaks had to be divided by twenty-five because, in addition to the two sons and three daughters in his own yurt, he had twenty foster children, most of whom had found their way to him as adolescents, and some as adults. (He had only four camels, each a gelding that he got when he was an old man, each in exchange for twenty-five fully-grown sheep rams. Those four, he used to say, belonged to nobody but him and his aged wife and were for carrying his equally aged yurt.)

Khylbangbaj was proverbially kind and above all, open-handed and generous. Anybody who no longer knew how to carry on in life struggled to reach his *ail*, threw himself at his feet, and asked for permission to call him Father. Khylbangbaj would immediately have the prostrate person stand, would have him fed, and would ask the members of his tribe who happened to be around to come and give witness about the person: Did he steal? Lie? Smoke? Drink? Was he violent? Was he known for any other vice? If all questions were answered in the supplicant's favour, my grandfather would say: Take him or her into your midst; let him be a brother or a sister to you; and treat him or her well. Only once or twice is he known to have rejected a supplicant. Everybody else was taken in and treated by him and the whole community like a child of the *daamal*. They would share shelter, kettle, and, of course, duties with the rest of the family, and receive their inheritance when they got married. Yes, *daamal*—that was his title, which eventually replaced his name among the Tuvans altogether. But by then the Kazakhs had arrived, and they kept calling him Khylbangbaj. *Daamal* probably meant chieftain in another, fancier language. It might have been Chinese because I have heard that *da* means 'grand' in Chinese, as in Grand Chief.

As the richest man's first-born son, my father must have entered adulthood as a powerful man. His most glorious stories dated back to those years. But then times changed, and anybody who had fat floating on top of the broth in his kettle was declared a *kulak* and thus an enemy of the people. Overnight, outsiders renamed my grandfather's many foster children his laborers. *Kulak*, from Russian, originally meant 'fist,' but carried the contemporary political meaning of 'wealthy landowner.' This punishing label was given to a herder-nomad who lived outside the contemporary world and its sense of time, and understood neither Russian nor politics. In this new world, a man, who some time earlier had been rejected by my grandfather because he had beaten a horse to death, now ran alongside omnipotent foreign revolutionaries and exposed people right and left with his two pricking and poking index fingers. Now this man was allowed to beat to death not only horses, but also people. Or shoot them. The phony little revolutionary soon carried a gun on his belt and used it extensively. But he never got the *daamal*. The *daamal*, already humiliated and frightened enough by what he had heard, escaped from him by dying just before the other showed up at his yurt to drive him, together with others, to their place of execution.

This is the setting of *The Blue Sky*. It was the time of greatest scarcity for our tribe and for nomads in general. The Thirties with their many arrests and executions still vividly gnawed at people's memory. The Forties, with the great World War and its wounds and consequences, were still with them—never before had people lived in such poverty and desperate straits as in those years. My father had donated the last remnants of his once large herd of horses to the front. It had turned a wealthy man into a poor one, but this gesture had given him some peace of mind. No longer could he be suspiciously eyed as a *kulak*. Yet his name retained the disastrous *baj*. Once he tried to drop the ending, but the newly powerful would have none of it: "Surely you aren't trying to cover over the tracks of your disgrace?" they shouted, and then: "These tracks will continue to give away who you are, who your children are, and then your children's children!" This referred to the fact that anybody who went to a government office with some request had to provide in writing his life story as well as his father's and grandfather's. Today—more than a decade and a half after the rule of terror ended—this infamous description of three life stories is still a requirement in any transactions with the government. Thus it was a given that I would have to thread my way painfully through accelerated times and different worlds.

Then slowly, but inexorably, and materially, life improved. The bitter, burning needs were alleviated. More and more often we got to eat flour. It was increasingly finely ground, and whiter. Millet was gradually replaced by rice. We came to know granulated sugar. First blue and green, then white cotton fabrics arrived in the yurt. We got to see banknotes, were allowed to carefully touch and even sniff them, and learned that we could get anything in return for them.

And we were told how to get the crinkling blue and red notes: by hunting wild animals and birds and delivering the kill to the district. Or by cutting tall, straight trees and rafting them down the river to the district center. Anybody wanting to get rich this way found that he could easily get whatever was needed to bring death to foxes and wolves, to rock partridges and gray partridges, to larch trees and pine trees: a gun, trap, poison, rope, saw, or axe. All these could be had unbelievably cheaply; they cost next to nothing. No doubt, the superpower's interests lay behind this easy availability, and invariably it was to that superpower that the spoils would go. Some found this situation beautiful, others ugly. Even those who found it beautiful thought: Killing animals—why not if it pays? But killing trees? No, never! So they left that to the Kazakhs, who had long mowed down the larch and pine forests closest to them.

As it turned out, people got rich quickly. But while the animal murderers were dealing in morsels, the tree murderers found themselves with such piles on their plate that they must have lost their senses: Overnight, they seemed to change into different people. Some modest socialist affluence—or, put more modestly, some appetizing whiff of it—had arrived in the remotest corner of the Mongolian state. But this judgment is based on a comparison of the present time with that in which *The Blue Sky* is set. Compared to the capital, Ulaanbaatar, time in the mountains stands still, dates back quite a few decades; and compared to the industrialized part of the world, even centuries.

This was the cost of the transformation: Gone were the forests. Gone the herds of moufflons, mountain goats, and other animals, and gone the coveys of rock partridges and gray partridges and other birds. The people stood as if changed from small and big children into small and big adults.

Nevertheless, one important point gives me comfort: That corner of the world that is my home, a full two thousand kilometers, an hour of the sun, five days by car, and decades if not millenia of progress removed from the capital Ulaanbaatar, has remained not the Wild, but the Gentle West of the Mongolian empire.

TRANSLATOR'S NOTE

In 2001, I fell in love with Galsan Tschinag's work. My first e-mail reached him two days before the fall of the Twin Towers, his reply to me two days after. He called my hope to translate *The Blue Sky* one day a small sun, shining from the West, and sent me a large herd of good spirits. Coming from a practising shaman, the wish for good spirits meant a great deal.

Two years later, I met Tschinag when he was in Germany on one of his many reading tours. Immediately he inquired about my family and began sharing the story of his. He spoke of life, death, family, love, and the heart. Before dinner, I learned about his horses, after dinner, about how as a shaman he heals people, even with a life-threatening injury inflicted by a horse. A bit of Mongolia had arrived in Germany. He takes some Altai soil with him wherever he goes.

In 2004, my husband and I went to visit Galsan in Mongolia. From the first moment, we were impressed by the hospitality. His children had been instructed to guide and take care of us. In Ulaanbaatar, they put us on the plane to Ölgiy, where we were met by another son who had spent two days coming down from the Altai to pick us up. From Ölgiy (elevation 1700 meters) we traveled by jeep toward the distant mountain range.

We were near the Russian border, and skirmishes in response to political borders that arbitrarily cross ancient tribal lands were common.

After hours of driving through the steppe and foothills—there are hardly any roads in Mongolia—we reached a windy mountain pass with a large *ovoo*, a cairn of sacrificial stones that marked the beginning of the traditional land of the Tuvans and, as the Mongolians say about this part of their country, the roof of the world. The air smelled of sage, and before us lay an awe-inspiring ocean of greenish-blue velvety mountain backs, broad valleys left behind by glaciers, and snow-covered peaks in the distance. 'Altai,' Galsan Tschinag has written, comes from 'ala,' multi-colored, and 'dag,' mountain. As the winds drove clouds across the sky, the mountains seemed to move under the changing patterns of sun and shadow, and it was easy to understand the Tuvans' veneration for the Altai.

For the next few hours we kept climbing. From time to time, a Kazakh or Tuvan yurt could be seen in the distance. In a few valleys, herders were making hay from small patches of green: struggling for every blade of grass. Toward evening we arrived in the Tsengelkhayrkhan mountain range. Towering over three yurts on a ridge at the end of a valley near the Black Lake was the 4000 meters-high sacred mountain. The Tuvans call it *Haarakan*, Great Mountain, because awe and respect forbid them to spell out the proper names of what is divine or dangerous. This was the furthest the jeep could go. To meet us, Galsan Tschinag had left the neighboring valley and ridden across a mountain through hours of a lashing rain storm. We saw him from afar astride his white horse waiting on the ridge. He welcomed us into a yurt especially made for us—a brand-new, shining white yurt we were invited to take back to North America. We were offered different kinds of cheese and fried dough, and invited to drink from the silver bowl that has come down to him from his ancestors—as has his snuff bottle, his silver flint and the silver sheath of the dagger he wears on his silk saffron belt over his blue velvet coat when he is in the Altai. His son came to play a concert for us on the horsehead fiddle. He had brought the mail with him from Ölgiy, which included an invitation by the President of the Republic of Tywa, who hoped Galsan Tschinag would join him for the celebrations of the republic's tenth anniversary; he would be offered a place of honour next to Putin. Clearly, we had arrived at the court of a prince. And we were honoured because translations build bridges—honoured by a man who is a most extraordinary bridge builder himself: As a shaman, he mediates between his community and the spirit world; as a chieftain, he connects Tuvans with each other; as a writer, he forges links between the oral tradition and epics of his people and the literate world outside; as a politician, he negotiates a future for his minority Tuvans among a sometimes hostile majority of Kazakhs and Mongolians; as a translator and teacher, he crosses, and enables others to cross, the linguistic borders of Tuvan, Kazakh, Mongolian, Russian, and German; and as a host, he opens his small yurt in the Altai, and his large yurt—the Altai and the steppe itself—to guests from abroad.

The next day, we continued our journey on horseback. Across steep, rocky terrain and a ridge more than 3000 meters high we rode for hours to reach the juniper valley, the summer pastures for a number of Tuvan and Kazakh families. There we watched Galsan Tschinag work as chieftain and shaman, and as host of a group of Europeans who, like us, had come to the Altai to learn about the Tuvans.

Every day Galsan took us to visit Tuvan and Kazakh families in the valley. Each had prepared a spread, mostly of meat and dairy products, but also of fried dough and sweets, and each offered us salted, buttery milk-tea and—since it was the foaling season—both fermented and distilled mare's milk. In one yurt, a whole wether had been slaughtered for the occasion. These were celebrations, but they clearly were also opportunities Galsan Tschinag created to braid together the Tuvan and Kazakh families who have to share the sparse resources of the land. He was always given the seat of honour at the North end of the yurt, and while the guests were offered delicacies such as the fatty tail of a sheep, he inquired—in Tuvan, Kazakh, or Mongolian—about the well-being of each family and their animals. As a result of four catastrophic winters and unusually dry summers, the nomads in the Altai had lost two-thirds of their herds in the previous decade. Galsan Tschinag's visits and the European visitors he has brought into the Altai for the last fifteen summers have created employment and income opportunities. We never left a yurt without him handing over a substantial stack of *tugrik* bills, but we also watched him engaging with every adult in the family; introducing the children to us; stroking, massaging, and caressing the sick and aged; praising (and translating into German) outstanding events and achievements; and making everybody feel encouraged and important.

In the process, we heard people's stories. We learned how mothers on horseback carry their baby's wooden cradle when the family moves: on a leather strap around the neck. More importantly, we learned how a family's history can be read from the second, thinner yak leather strap stretched across the cradle. It allows visitors to avoid asking painful questions and instead find gentle and empathetic words. For every birth of a boy, a sheep's right ankle bone is tied to the strap, for every girl, a left one. For every child that has died, the bone is removed, but the knot remains.

Bones connect life and death, the material and the spiritual. They were read by our host, by the shaman who provided guidance and support, and who taught us to read in the book of nature. A rock face, so forbidding from a distance, shows fracture lines from close up: nothing is forever, everything changes. Birds that breed their young at a lake near the foot of *Haarakan's* glacier grieve when one of the couple dies. The shaman translated: love is the key to life, and the cause of suffering. Do as the birds.

The morning we started our two-day trip back to Ölgiy, people gathered to say farewell. Each was blessed by Galsan Tschinag, the shaman, with the traditional sprinkling of milk. And because my husband and I were the first North Americans to come to the Tuvan land in the High Altai, we were given special gifts to take home. The Cold War is ending, people had repeatedly said to us in the days before. When we laid our customary three stones on the *ovoo*, we had reason to be grateful indeed.

Like the birds Galsan Tschinag had referred to, I had embarked on my own journey to the top of the world. I returned with the shaman's blessings to complete the translation of his important first novel into English. I want to thank Galsan Tschinag and his people for generously receiving us into their lives, and Galsan himself for discussing his text and my translation with me. I am also very grateful to Hiro Boga and Ron Smith from Oolichan Books, and to Daniel Slager from Milkweed Editions, for their careful and insightful editorial suggestions; to Malaspina University-College for supporting my work; and to my husband Jonathan for having shared my journey half way round the world to bring the project to completion.

Before I left, Galsan made one final observation: "I am convinced that our corner could quickly turn into a Karabakh or Kosovo, if in a country such as ours, with a colorful mix of peoples and a leadership that glorifies violence and war, the Tuvan people were to glorify their own and denigrate their neighbors' cultures." Bridges have to be built from both sides of a river, though. While Galsan Tschinag promotes foreign-language learning among the Tuvans, he also gives one manuscript a year for publication, royalty-free, to a Mongolian publisher, hoping to sow the seeds of respect for Tuvan culture among his fellow Mongolians. His stories, he says about all his books, are not his stories alone: they are the stories of his people.

And they are stories for the world.

GALSAN TSCHINAG, whose name in his native Tuvan language is Irgit Schynykbaj-oglu Dshurukuwaa, was born in the early forties in Mongolia. From 1962 until 1968 he studied at the University of Leipzig, where he adopted German as his written language. Under an oppressive Communist regime he became a singer, storyteller, and poet in the ancient Tuvan tradition. As the chief of Tuvans in Mongolia, Tschinag led his people, scattered under Communist rule, back in a huge caravan to their original home in the high Altai Mountains. Tschinag is the author of more than thirty books, and his work has been translated into many languages. He lives alternately in the Altai, Ulaanbaatar, and Europe.

KATHARINA ROUT studied German and English literature and received her PhD from the University of Münster. She teaches English and German literatures at Malaspina University-College in Nanaimo, British Columbia.

MORE FICTION FROM MILKWEED EDITIONS

Katya
Sandra Birdsell

My Lord Bag of Rice:
New and Selected Stories
Carol Bly

The Tree of Red Stars
Tessa Bridal

Crossing Bully Creek
Margaret Erhart

Ordinary Wolves
Seth Kantner

Hunting Down Home
Jean McNeil

Swimming in the Congo
Margaret Meyers

Cracking India
Bapsi Sidhwa

Montana 1948
Larry Watson

To order books or for more information, contact Milkweed at
(800) 520-6455 or visit our Web site (www.milkweed.org).

MILKWEED ⬯ EDITIONS

Founded in 1979, Milkweed Editions is one of the largest independent, nonprofit literary publishers in the United States. Milkweed publishes with the intention of making a humane impact on society, in the belief that good writing can transform the human heart and spirit. Within this mission, Milkweed publishes in four areas: fiction, nonfiction, poetry, and children's literature for middle-grade readers.

JOIN US

Milkweed depends on the generosity of foundations and individuals like you, in addition to the sales of its books. In an increasingly consolidated and bottom-line-driven publishing world, your support allows us to select and publish books on the basis of their literary quality and the depth of their message. Please visit our Web site (www. milkweed.org) or contact us at (800) 520-6455 to learn more about our donor program.

MILKWEED EDITIONS
EDITOR'S CIRCLE

Interior design and typesetting
by Percolator

Typeset in Anziano

Printed on Rolland Enviro 100
(100% post consumer waste)
by Friesens Corporation